THE TOWER OF POWER

COMMODORE B. CLARK

PublishAmerica
Baltimore

First printing

At the specific preference of the author, PublishAmerica allowed this work to remain exactly as the author intended, verbatim, without editorial input.

ISBN: 1-4241-4020-X
PUBLISHED BY PUBLISHAMERICA, LLLP
www.publishamerica.com
Baltimore

Printed in the United States of America

DEDICATION

For my precious mother
and all mothers like her

To Allison Walker
Best wishes always
Commodore Clark
2-07

PROLOGUE

I grew up in a community where Black men chose to put on a demeanor of cool. It was the cool school era when jazz and be-bop were kings and the hip *thang* was being cool by not showing your hand. It was an era—the late '40s and '50s—when you shrouded yourself in a mystique of aloofness so you could appear and disappear at will, an era when you seemed to others to be into something – but what?

I couldn't have imagined how my cool world would turn hot in the next decades, or that I'd be called into a revolution at a radio station in Detroit. This is the story of what happened at WTOP, and more than that, it's a journey of a man who was forged by his times.

CHAPTER ONE

1953. I'd returned from the Korean War to a nation of segregated neighborhoods where WASP entitlements and privileges were normal, families stuck to their own ethnic groups, and everyone was expected to work hard. It was a time of blind faith in the status quo, when the "silent generation" heard no evil, saw no evil, and spoke no evil. For a patriotic post-war generation, the motto was "love of country, right or wrong," and the majority society asserted "I'm free, white and twenty-one," knowing the implications of that phrase. Negroes (as we were called then) couldn't sing "God Bless America" with the real joyous passion of Kate Smith, but no one was noticing, back then.

By '57, we lived uneasily in a time when injustice done to Negroes anywhere touched off a rippling psychological effect of injustice done to Negroes everywhere. Just two years before, we'd heard news of the torture and murder of Emmett Till in '55, and in that same year, the arrest of Rosa Parks for violating the Montgomery, Alabama segregation laws by refusing to give up her seat on a bus to a white man. It was at that time that a little known minister, Dr. Martin Luther King, Jr., emerged as head of the Montgomery Improvement Association, which was formed to strike all city buses. After 381 days of Negroes walking in pride and refusing to ride in shame, the bus strike ended successfully. All of us throughout the States who felt a kinship to the movement rejoiced!

That was the beginning. With the enactment of the Fair Employment Practices Act, a few Negroes were hired to work in some private companies. In nearby Inkster, Michigan, WDDD became one of the first licensed Negro-owned radio stations. Suddenly, WTOP, "The Tower," an ethnic radio station located among the skyscrapers of beautiful downtown Detroit, had competition.

And so it was, through the efforts of the Urban League that I became the first Negro hired by The Tower as a "Merchandising and Public Relations Manager." I had no illusions that the only reason they put me on the staff was to give the station some credibility in the Negro market.

In this same period, the Announcers' Union was informed that a new automation system was being installed to improve program operations. But it would require only three announcers instead of nine. Uncertainty spread among the jocks – who would monitor the logs and announce the station breaks? So by the time I arrived, an atmosphere of apprehension and distrust was palpable.

In the hallways I heard snippets, mostly ethnic directors blaming other ethnic programmers. When I'd walk into a room the conversation would hush. No doubt about it – when I wasn't around, the same kind of backbiting was being directed at me. Feuds, rumors and innuendos steamed in a pressure cooker of mistrust. Finally, the announcers called a strike.

Through it all, my mindset was based on faith, in the old Negro tradition. I adopted an invisible, perpetual mask, as we'd learned to wear in a white work environment. Among other rules, it required a smile when you don't feel like smiling, and apologizing when you've done no wrong, always concealing your true sentiments. We all did that to be accepted, for survival, and for our personal security. I did no wrong that would reflect on my people. All I wanted was a job in which I could move forward to secure a comfortable life for my future family and myself. I observed, but rarely made a comment. Along with this mask, I combined street smarts. My precious mother, who my sisters and I called Mother Dear, had taught me patience. Thus I managed to circumvent the turbulence and survived three bosses who got the ax in my first three months at the station.

In the fall of '61, with the announcer's strike still unsettled, a pall fell over The Tower. Earnings were down in all foreign-language segments. The spot-sales within Negro programming were spotty at best. A few of the time segments sold went to legitimate churches, but most were bought by "jack-legged preachers" who profited by hawking their dreams during their Saturday or Sunday night programs to their unsophisticated audience in exchange for contributions through the mail. Rumors raged that major cutbacks were coming.

Gerald T. Bonner, the General Manager and Sales Director, had floated a warning that he was going to cut anyone who added additional expenses to The Tower's overhead. My grapevine whispered that meant one of the office girls and me. Now, I always maintained a friendly relationship with the ladies, treating them with respect. Maybe that came from growing up with four older sisters. And, in time, those relationships were well repaid in information. So when Karl Kruger met with Bonner, I eventually found out what went down.

Karl had been brought into sales to sell the German programs and had a chance to sell others if he could. A deacon in his church, he exploited his position to handle the jack-legged preachers, as if it attested to his God-fearing nature. A cloudy gray hat, never removed, covered his baldhead, though strands of dingy blond hair strayed at the nape of his neck. He'd begun wearing that hat everyday when he worked at a small town newspaper in Ohio, embarrassed by getting bald. Along with that hat, he wore the same cheap gray suit every day he'd worked at The Tower, his baggy pants thin with a shine at his wide, flat rear, worn out from all his time whirling in his seat by the phone.

That day, Karl expected Bonner to confirm he was cutting me. But Bonner surprised him. An attractive colored lady from the

NAACP had come in to talk with him about their campaign, Bonner said, seeking cooperation from companies who would hire some Negroes. To defend the station, Bonner had used my name, and now he was afraid that without me the NAACP might accuse him of discrimination and start picketing the station like they were doing the bank down the street. Then Bonner shocked Karl, revealing he was thinking of giving me a chance in sales.

"The Buhl isn't going to let you bring colored into sales," Karl shot back.

The Buhl was the company that owned WTOP and various stations elsewhere. Its office was only blocks away from The Tower, but they weren't normally involved in day-to-day business. Still, Karl invoked The Buhl to fend off any competition; their position on race was well known.

Bonner said under the present circumstances he didn't have much choice. Karl thought a moment then shrugged it off. As hard as it was to sell time there, he figured putting me in sales would be the same as canning me.

"I doubt he'll be able to make his draw in three months, and if not, you'll have a legitimate reason to squeeze him out."

"That's the same thought I had," Bonner said. "Plus, by that time the NAACP campaign should be over."

Bonner assured Karl that he was still in charge. He could give me whatever leads he wanted – or not give them to me. Bonner would back him, no matter what. Just keep in mind not to let it look like they were conspiring.

But I didn't know any of that when I called The Tower and got a message to come to Bonner's office the following day. I looked out the window at the hawk gusting, howling, striking people's heads as they bent their backs to plow through it. I turned to the mirror, preparing to go out, and slicked down my black, curly hair, satisfied with my well-kept mustache, and my face that a woman once described as cream'n'coffee. Standing six-foot-one, I'd molded my body with weight-lifting through my high school All-City gridiron days and the army's daily dozens, and still had the body of an athlete, at thirty-one. With care, I put on one of my three-piece suits, my Swiss watch and diamond ring, and in the mirror I saw a gentleman, distinguished from those around me.

Bonner had been a captain in the Canadian Air Force during World War II, and had problems adjusting to civilian life after it. Used to giving orders, he couldn't find another job where he could order people around. He came to the Motor City and worked at several general market radio stations, but never gained the attention he'd hungered for. Moreover, rumors had him on his way out of the business before he latched onto The Tower.

When he arrived as General Manager and Sales Director, he iced five employees, so he was back in the saddle again. His stiff military bearing and his steel gray eyes, alternately trusting and suspicious, hadn't made him an easy man to approach.

I'd stayed out of his way. I knew from past experience with my former bosses that only when Bonner caught hell with his presentations in New York and found himself in serious trouble would he, for his own survival, set aside his arrogance and come to me for advice on the Negro market. Through the years, Bonner had permitted himself to be schooled on two important national accounts, arming himself with just enough market info to keep them on the books.

Meanwhile I got over on my own, representing The Tower at social functions, creating promotions, and establishing a merchandising format. My work proved invaluable to Bonner, so the tenuous beginning of our relationship had become somewhat acceptable. Of course, I knew I was only Bonner's advisor, his station's window-dressing to be pulled out and showcased to any client who challenged the station's authenticity in the Negro market. But I'd prepared myself to assume that role with dignity, respecting others, and myself never demanding anything directly.

Still, I had my strategies. I'd heard the rumor that cutbacks might include me, so I'd gone to an NAACP meeting and sought out Grace Washington. I had no expectations beyond lighting a fire under Bonner to keep my job safe. I simply asked Grace to approach

Bonner and inquire about the number of Negroes working there. After her meeting, she'd called me.

I knew only that much as I plowed through the wind past the Madison Theatre to the revolving doors of The Tower. At 35 floors, it was the fourth tallest building in Detroit after the Fisher Building, the Penobscot and The Buhl. High above, the transmitter pierced the sky over the letters WTOP.

I paused outside Bonner's door. With memories of employees I'd seen come and go, I stiffened, then knocked, announced myself, and prepared for whatever.

Bonner stood inside, impeccably groomed from his silver-gray hair down to his spit-shined black Bostonian kicks. He was shorter than me, medium height, with thick, dark brows and a keen nose above a thin mustache frosted with gray. In his fifties, he was more than twenty years my senior. He beckoned me to a chair, and sat behind his large desk. He looked troubled, strained; something about the man, beneath his proper manners, hinted at something hidden. It was a kind of thing I couldn't put my finger on, and it made me uneasy being alone in Bonner's company. Maybe the problem was Bonner's memory lapse, which occurred often enough on important issues that we'd addressed together over time, that led me to wonder if Bonner hadn't been as sincere as he claimed, or if he was testing the reliability of my own recall.

As the windows rattled in the wind, I fixed my eyes on Bonner, waiting, wondering how long Bonner would assume his worried pose, and to what extent I even wanted his sympathy if he was going to lower the boom.

"I'm sorry," Bonner finally said, shaking his head with a heavy sigh of bewilderment. "I just don't know. I don't! The Buhl must think I'm a magician. I got nothing to work with, yet they expect me to make this station a million bucks."

I said nothing. After four years, I still didn't know the people at The Buhl company headquarters. Neither did they know me personally. What could I say? Besides, these money problems were old news.

"Don't pay me any mind, my boy. You're the only one here I can take into my confidence. I've had it up to here with The Buhl."

His body quivering in fury, he paused for a moment, his gray eyes flaring. He went on to complain that it's not enough that he has to contend with all the foreign-language directors and their problems, with the station announcer's strike, with his colored personalities, and with the pettiness of some employees around there to keep the damn station on the air. "No, that's not enough!" he said. "I also have to contend with interference from those screwballs at The Buhl. I should tell them to take this thankless job and shove it! Anyway," he exhaled, trying to shake off his anger, "that's not the problem I wanted to discuss with you."

His gaze became more intense as he smoothed over his desk pad, a gesture he usually indulged before getting to his real point.

"You probably know that sales are way off. I have a piss-poor sales staff. I wanted to let Henry Kolinsky go, but The Buhl said he's too important to the sales of the Polish programs. I don't agree. He's just a crybaby. He's always going over to The Buhl complaining about my handling of things. Damn, if I wasn't the type of man I am, I'd give him a couple of good socks on that troublemaking mouth of his."

His tone softened as he went on, "But that's not what I wanted to discuss." He leaned back in his tall leather chair, as if evaluating his performance. "I've gotten in touch with some people in the trade as you'd suggested some time back. After talking to them and some of their referrals, my thoughts came back to you.

"Except for the information you've shared with me, I know very little about Negroes. Frankly, I'm uncomfortable around some. Now don't take that wrong," he was quick to add. "There have been many whites I've not been comfortable around in my lifetime. But that's different. I can be miserable around them and show it, and not be accused of being biased because of color. But with Negroes, it's almost impossible to dislike one without being accused of being a white bigot. Do you follow what I'm saying?"

I was growing impatient. I'd heard excuses from white bosses enough to know it didn't make sense to answer. Probably he was asking me to get him off the hook, assuage any guilt, and I couldn't do that. So I merely nodded.

"You've taught me all I know about the colored market," he resumed. "And it works! You're blessed with several pluses going for you: the ability to think clearly, perseverance, a good background in sales, and a superior knowledge of your market. You're a credit to your race. You're the man Karl and I want to see in my sales department. How about it?"

He put on a welcoming smile.

My mouth felt dry. In those moments of silence, I imagined myself looking like a dumbfounded country fool just off the train. There'd been rumors circulated by the jocks that ownership didn't want a Negro in sales because the ad agencies wouldn't accept him. The offer came as a complete surprise, no rumor, and no nothing until this moment. And while it was something I'd privately longed to do, I'd all but given up on ever becoming a salesman there. Plainly, I was speechless.

"That's all right," Bonner said. "Don't give your answer now. Take some time and think it over. And please don't let this on to anyone. I want to get you started before anyone knows. In a couple of days let's sit down and talk more about it, okay?"

Even if I hadn't been caught unaware, what could I say? It's not like I really had a choice in the matter, and it brought on mixed feelings. Of course, it was good news. It could be the stepping-stone to that comfortable future I'd always envisioned. I'd been helping others with their sales, and now I'd get a chance to do it myself. I knew all the fundamentals of salesmanship – how to prospect, how to make an approach, how to make a presentation, how to handle rebuttals, and how to close. I'd done some sales back when I was hustling insurance right after the war. Yet, now, I was uncomfortable. Why? Was it that I didn't know if I could trust Bonner? Was I uncomfortable with change? Was I afraid of failing? More than that, I suspected that the weight of my success or failure would bear heavily on the chances of others of color to get into the business.

If I was to take the position, I needed a full picture of ownership to understand what I was really selling. I wanted facts, not rumors from lower-level staff trying to ingratiate themselves under the pretense of having inside information. The Buhl's stationery listed fourteen small mid-western radio stations of which WTOP was its largest source of revenue, but I had inkling the company was more powerful than that.

At Detroit's Main Library across from the Historical Museum in the city's Cultural Center, I researched The Buhl and discovered the company also owned several newspapers throughout Michigan, an interest in a major market television station, and a bank in Detroit. I was flabbergasted. By the shoddiness of The Tower's operation, I never imagined the parent company's scope and influence. So, after two days of mulling over the questions I'd posed to myself, I figured if I could stay on top of my market's pulse, there'd be no limits to the business I could get. I had to succeed.

So I accepted the salesman position. At my desk, I studied the account list and the rate card Bonner gave me. Then I checked out the broadcast schedule. It showed eighty-eight hours per week of Negro programming, with ten different foreign languages to be sold on their corresponding shows arranged throughout the day and night. These, along with the Negro shows, were my scope of sales.

Using the account list, I made phone calls, but I soon discovered that almost none of the accounts were aware of the station. In fact, a number of accounts no longer even existed. After days of working steadily from the list, it was apparent: the list was as jive as my squeaky chair.

"What kind of shit is this?" I muttered to myself, threw down the list, and slouched back in that rickety chair.

I try not to get down, so in that moment, I reached for memories of being a child, loved and protected, and I thought about my mother. I was just a three-month-old baby when my father died, leaving her alone to be both mother and father to my four sisters and me. I could picture her sewing our clothes, stitching cotton dresses for the girls, taking a used coat and re-making it for me. I smiled, picturing an old photo of me at five in that coat with a cap, standing proudly in short pants and knee socks at her side. I remembered her simple, tasteful bead necklace and the small hoops of her gold earrings. I was blessed to have the kind of mother who'd taught me to be patient, to observe, to listen, to think, and then analyze situations before making final judgments. She had died in the year before I went to work at the station, but I felt her with me.

I straightened and made a resolve to keep my cool and not allow anything to get to me or get in the way of being the best I could be. I tossed the list and set out to pound the streets. It took days and nights of pushing before I brought in my first contract. And though it was inconsequential in volume and dollars, it was a lift for me, a start.

I turned my attention to the upcoming political race where money would come fast and up-front. It was my first opportunity to participate in this lucrative part of the business, and I was naive about the dog-eat-dog competition that rose between the salesmen in the absence of assigned candidates. To be first on the scene meant nothing. The business was credited to whoever brought in the contract with the money. Besides regular ad agency business, the challenge was the rat race of dogging the candidates or their reps to sign and give up the money before some other salesman came along.

At the end of that election season, I'd survived the big push. It had been an exhausting experience, and every dollar I earned had been hard fought. At my desk, I felt played out. But I didn't get a chance to relax. Realizing I hadn't fallen on my face, Karl Kruger was turning openly antagonistic.

Karl wouldn't even touch me with a handshake. To others at The Tower, he was a conniving, abrasive hanger-on who wouldn't be anything without Bonner's backing. The little business he had brought to the German programs was sloppy at best, and the German program director had even asked that Karl be canned.

But Karl had developed a friendship with the vice president and controller, Edward Butler, and that led to another layer of intrigue. Bonner saw Butler as his archenemy, the focus of his insecurity and paranoia about The Buhl. So Bonner had made Karl his mole to keep him informed about the controller's moves. For Karl's services as a spy, Bonner gave him control of all the church segments. Bonner even put Karl in charge when he was out of town, and in charge of all incoming leads.

So Karl was halfway in bed with Bonner. But little did Bonner know that the other half of Karl's bed was shared with Edward Butler. Yes, Karl was Butler's mole as well, playing both ends against the middle whenever it suited him.

It always suited Karl to keep me down, or claim my successes for himself. Late in the election campaign, when I'd turned in a healthy schedule of political ads, Karl was in Bonner's office with my paperwork.

I'd come to give Rose, Bonners' secretary, a box of chocolates for her birthday. She was out to lunch with some of the other ladies, so I lay the box on her desk. As I turned to go back to my office, I heard Bonner talking to Karl.

"Find me a good reason to turn this business over to you and I'll do it," Bonner told him. "Otherwise, what kind of a man would I look like in his eyes?"

"I'm not concerned with his opinion of you," Karl answered. "I've done many favors for you by keeping Ed Butler and The Buhl off your back. Besides, I'm the one who went and picked up the copy. It was my turn for a lead. I don't know how he got it. Maybe one of the girls told him about it. As hard as it is to sell this fucking time, I'm not about to lose something that's mine."

Karl had raised his voice so I could hear enough of this to keep quiet, waiting for how Bonner would deal with him. Of course, Bonner knew that Karl kept the best leads for himself, and figured that was all right, as long as it didn't create any big quibbles. Now Bonner tried to sound conciliatory.

"Karl," Bonner said, "you're a good man to have around. You're a friend, a good family man with six mouths to feed. That's why I put you in a position to be the top salesman. I believe I've done more for you than you have for me." Then Bonner's voice grew tense, "So don't you ever throw that Buhl business in my face again. If you want this commission so much, go settle it on your own."

I was back at my desk when Karl barged in.

"Boy! Is this the way you repay me after it was me who got you into sales? Is it? Is it?" He shook his index finger at my nose.

That did it. My cool was blown, overwhelmed with indignation. All I could hear was "Boy!" reverberating in my head, cutting across my nerves and senses. It wasn't so much Karl's use of "Boy" that raised my wrath, because I'd outgrown my sensitivity to its use long ago. It was the way Karl said it, with such sudden, bitter arrogance that left me spinning. The fool, I thought, the crazy, dumb fool doesn't know who he's messing with.

I rose, pushing back my seat with a foot, slamming the door closed with a flip of my hand. For a moment, I forgot all the tolerance, all the polish and all the patience I'd gained since my teens, the discipline I'd developed to deal with people unemotionally, correctly.

"Mutha..." I caught myself quickly and swallowed hard not to say that word that was forcing its way out through my rage. I felt a gust of energy and I wanted to strike back. But the mask I'd always worn at work restrained me; I knew full well if I unleashed my verbal artillery it would be too vehement and I wouldn't be able to function here afterwards. I felt helplessly naked, stripped of tongue, arms and fist. I knew I would have to think, and then purge myself of this sensation so I wouldn't explode. I did the only thing I could do, short of fisticuffs, to show Karl I was intact and not about to cave in. I reverted to a childhood ploy. I stood firm, saying nothing, and fixed an icy, hypnotic stare, through which I vented anger into Karl's eyes.

Silence fell around us. Karl's puffed up chest began to deflate. His body wavered, and as his menacing disposition gave way, I saw his expression change from a mad dog to a befuddled puppy uncertain what was on his master's mind. I'd stared the sucker down and had put him in a box "like jack." And I wasn't about to spring him until I was good and ready.

"As long as you know me, don't ever approach me in that fashion again," I said, with tight control. "Furthermore, I don't know what you're talking about, and at the moment, I don't care."

"You're not going to take food out of my family's mouth," Karl retorted, his voice thick.

"Just what do you mean by that?"

"You know damn well. You stole a political commission from right under my nose."

I heard him out, listening for any shred of fact. But the more he went on, challenging my integrity, the more I was sure the clown was out to lunch. I'd worked hard for that piece of business. I'd called on the agency, initiated the order, got the contract, picked up the copy from a recording studio, and had turned in the order, all over a period of two weeks. I had the records to back me up.

As Karl spewed his lies I imagined going upside the sucker's head. Never mind that Karl weighed more. I still knew plenty of tricks from the street. But then, I thought, what utter nonsense. All that would accomplish would be getting me iced. And it would make me as much a fool as Karl. No, I'd take the dispute to Bonner for his judgment, certain that I could prove the facts.

Prepared, feeling confident, I sat in Bonner's office and handed him copies of my work sheets covering the time in question. Step by step I slowly detailed my involvement. I made no attempt at salesmanship – it wasn't necessary. I merely demonstrated the evidence – contacts, extension numbers, dates, times and comments. After ten minutes or so, certain I'd made my case, I pushed back in my seat.

I watched Bonner fidget over the reports as if he was contriving ways to handle the situation, hanging in doubt. But why? Everything was clearly spelled out.

"Well, Karl," Bonner finally looked up from the reports, "what do you have to say on your behalf?"

Anxiously, I anticipated Karl's lies so I could tear them to shreds with my records.

The whole time I spoke, Karl slouched, his beer-belly like the hump on a camel's back, doodling on a notepad, unconcerned with the evidence. Now he stopped doodling and cleared his throat. With a crooked smile, he said leisurely, "Jerry, for all the years I've been in this business, I believe it's common practice that a phone confirmation is as good as a signed contract. Am I right or wrong?"

That was the opening Bonner needed to give himself a way out. Bonner pretended to search his memory a few moments before he affirmed sanctimoniously, "You're right. You're absolutely right about that."

True, I didn't have their years in the business or their experience in office politics, but Mother Dear hadn't raised any fools. I hadn't wanted to think Bonner was a bigot, and it was inconceivable that they could think of me as stupid. Yet I felt the two were laughing at my expense, as if I was a befuddled clown in the center of a circus ring. No way would I have believed the way this cheap conspiracy unfolded if I hadn't been present to see it played out on me. They had me in a bind. I couldn't complain to The Buhl, as other salesmen might have done. I was no more than a name that showed up on a commission sheet to them, a peon with no clout. Besides, the dollar amount involved wouldn't be worth the bother to them. Nevertheless, a principle was at stake.

I started to get up and leave in mute protest at the betrayal, but on second thought, I couldn't let them off the hook that easily. The least I could do is try to prick their conscience, and get a better fix on my position.

I asked Bonner if he accepted Karl's premise that he actually received the so-called phone confirmation, even though he couldn't provide the name of his contact or anything. "In other words, are you consenting to Karl's words over my facts?"

"I have no reason to question him," Bonner replied summarily without the slightest compunction.

That did it! Bonner's reply was so empty and transparent that I needed all my strength to maintain my cool. In less time than it took to present my case, they'd put me in a trick-bag, and struck me out with a curve for which I couldn't have prepared. And I could do absolutely nothing but fight back my rage and turn my hard work over to Karl.

The position Bonner took against me left me deeply wounded.

Why should I keep trying so hard in this job when my progress would be impeded, no matter what I did? I searched my soul, and vowed not to let them push me out, but to get payback one day, though I didn't yet know how.

Fueled by anger and an indomitable will to succeed, I hit the streets. I kept busy servicing a couple of accounts, making collections, and writing the type of copy that spoke directly to my market. But that just wasn't enough to prove my worth as a salesman. So I changed my approach. With a quiet sense of purpose, I hit the smaller ad agencies, the nightclubs, the promotional business, and the auto risk insurance companies. Three months into my new approach, I'd realized a good portion of what I'd set out to accomplish. By then I'd repaid my overdraw and was making a small commission.

I'd foiled Karl and Bonner's scheme to drive me out. But I was still low man on the totem pole, and knew that only a big account would gain me the respect from The Buhl and get me where I wanted to go.

CHAPTER TWO

Over the next months, I picked up business throughout the community – a community in the throes of change. I realized the way to stay on top of my market's pulse, nationally and locally, was to become active in its drive for civil rights, participating in the people's concerns. The atmosphere was disquieting. People who had been drained of self-respect from years of oppression had become worn down by the segregated society, and some were just plain tired of it all. Except for working within the system to improve education, employment, housing, and social justice, assimilation seemed utterly irrelevant.

There were a few high-and-mighty groups who felt they were above the masses, people with economic security who chose to ignore the problems of most people of color. But what was most troubling were how many had lost faith in America, who were filled with bitterness and hatred, and were willing to do whatever, even resort to violence. The community really needed a commonality to bring it together.

In the summer of '63, I quickly finished working with a client in a rush to get downtown before traffic tied me up. At The Tower, I dropped off my business, then raced downstairs, and joined the mile-long sea of humanity walking down Woodward Avenue.

Dr. Martin Luther King and other dignitaries were at its head in what was billed the Freedom Walk that ended at Cobo Hall with a rally. By now, Dr. King was widely known as the leader of the non-violent civil rights movement. Frequently, he'd come to speak in Detroit, a union site with many influential leaders, both Negro and white. Many in our community revered him, especially older folks who had struggled for justice and parity over the years, and respected by some outside, as well.

Addressing an overflowing audience, the second largest crowd that had ever rallied in the city, he delivered his renowned "I have a dream" speech that was the genesis for the one he later gave at the giant march on Washington. Those from the community who'd been fortunate to get inside to hear his message of hope and brotherhood left in jubilation, eager to tell everyone how they'd been inspired. What a day! Dr. King had reaffirmed the people's faith, and it was just what the community needed. That speech became a never-ending topic in barbershops, beauty salons, markets – all the places ordinary people went every day.

However, on the streets and in poolrooms, younger brothers and sisters had a different reaction. Sure, they gave Dr. King his "prospers," but they'd tell you they weren't strong on that "turn the other cheek shit". Malcolm X, the Black Muslim leader who repudiated King's non-violent philosophy, was closer to how they felt. With no sugarcoating, Malcolm taught if someone strikes you, by any means necessary, strike him back as hard as you can.

Many in the older generation, who still couched their feelings behind masks in public, were uncomfortable with Malcolm airing their hidden sentiments so directly. But to the young brothers, he reaffirmed their manhood. Despite the differences within the community, a prudent consensus emerged: The people embraced both leaders, agreeing both spoke the truth. Through debating the contrary philosophies, the previously quiet community was awakening to its historic struggle for human dignity and rights.

Still puffed up with pride weeks after Dr. King's appearance, I left The Tower at the end of a hectic Friday. I was looking forward to my last appointment of the week, which would be my biggest sale yet, a weekly remote broadcast on which I'd worked for two months.

As I turned my ride onto Hancock, then swung up John R, an incredible joy was emerging from deep within. Twilight was seeping into darkness as I parked a couple of blocks away from the eastside strip, which held three blocks of nightspots. John R was alive as always. The mild wind touching my cheeks energized me, and I strutted along the one-way street with a tempered bounce and swagger, greeting "Hey now" to anyone catching my eye. High on life, the mood brought back my college days.

Sometimes after classes I'd hang out on the streets, hearing their beat, feeling like I was caressed by the rhythm that made them flow with such dazzle. It was the kind of atmosphere that had given me a sense of manly hipness, where I learned to "check my checkers and watch my watchers." Years ago, I'd even hung out along this very strip, being cool, leaning back in my Father'n'Son kicks, shuckin'n'jivin with the young players, talkin' sweet-talk to the ladies while delighting them with my hip dancing displays.

Back then; I delighted in being called "Strict-business" because I was a college boy who had the tendency to counter the b.s.ers when they went too far over the edge. Nevertheless, with all considered, my good sense and my knowledge of street hustles and the kind of life that pivoted around them stopped me short of getting seriously involved in its culture. First and foremost, Mother Dear taught me to respect my home and myself. Her influence, which set my moral and spiritual balance, ultimately was what kept me out of harm's way. I wanted more than this. A hustle, yes, but one coming through a legitimate means.

The "hawgs" (Cadillac's) and the "deuce-and-a-quarters" (Buick Electra 225s), each polished to sheen, snatched me out of my memories. The players were already out checking their traps, careening stiffly behind their steering wheels, tapping their horns lightly in greeting, being cool. Up ahead, Barbecue Red, a young player, stood on the corner talking loud and drawing a crowd with his colorful line of b.s. Nearby, Peaches'n'Cream, two ladies-of-the-night, stood sexily by the side of the defunct Flame Show Bar, leering at the passing rides and ready to trot. A ragtop canary-yellow hawg slowed and set in front of the Frolic Show Bar, its horn playing "Mary had a little lamb," attracting a gaping crowd.

I heard the sounds of doo-wappin' emanating from three teenage boys arrayed on the stoop of a brownstone across the street. Walking by the next row house, I waved at the two teen girls on the stoop whom I'd known as kids hula-hooping across the sidewalk. I passed the Chesterfield Bar, overhearing Mutt'n'Jeff, two plain-clothes ofay (white) cops, trying to talk jive talk out the sides of their mouths, but it lacked the rhythm, the flare, and the flatness. I snickered to myself at their bungling ineptness, and crossed at Garfield Street, dodging the double-parked rides that awaited the sure-footed hot-tomalley-man, dressed all in white with a chef's hat.

When I opened the door of the Garfield Lounge, the boisterous voices, laughter, and the music from the jukebox charged out at me like a back draft from a fire suddenly fueled with air. I removed my shades, focused my eyes, and, standing inside the entrance, raked over the patrons. The bar lights glistened off the "Sugar Ray do's" of the cats draped around the bar, their "Mr. B collars" cramping their necks. It was chicken in the basket night, which usually brought in the black and tan, trendy in-crowd. I could see the professionals, the salesmen, the athletes, the players and their ladies, the self-styled political pundits, the socialites and the curious ones talking together in raspy tones above the clamor. But no Randolph, the owner I'd come to see.

I greeted the waitress, who went to fetch Randolph, said hello to the bartender, and gave up some skin to others I knew at the bar. It wasn't long before the waitress returned, saying, "Mr. Randolph will be tied up for a while, but he asked you to wait." She offered me a drink, which I declined – I'm careful to stay alert when I'm doing business. I noticed Wilbur Parker, a potential insurance client, coming in with some others, and I waved to him, staying positive as I waited. I checked my watch: five-thirty on the nose.

Wilbur came over, looking worried. "Why didn't you return my partner's call? I called your office to tell you Lee was pissed and for you to get crackin', but you'd left. Now my partner's sold on giving his business to your competition, WDDD, instead. You better get over to the office tomorrow morning, if you want in on this."

I didn't know what Wilbur was talking about. I hadn't received any call from the partner, Mr. Lee. And I didn't have much confidence in Wilbur Parker. I'd put in plenty of time selling to him, only to find out later he didn't have the final say. Besides, I'd written off working Saturdays – it wasn't productive. But I wasn't about to burn bridges, so I explained I wasn't told about the call, and walked him back to his company.

Still waiting for Randolph, I took a seat at a back table in the shadows. I removed a folder of proposals from my attaché case, and pretended to browse through them, though I could barely see in the dim lighting. Engrossed in thoughts of the proposed remotes and what they could bring, I didn't even hear myself being paged until the waitress was in front of me. "Mr. Randolph is waiting on the line for you," she pointed to the front where Mack, the bartender, was impatiently waving the house receiver above his head.

Folks now stood two abreast at the bar; most of the tables were occupied. I got myself together, consulted my watch again, went over and took the receiver.

"Randolph, it's six-fifteen."

Randolph apologized and asked if I'd prepared the proposals. Eagerly, I told him yes – the two we'd spoken about, and another in case those were too costly. Randolph got right to the point – though he hadn't had the guts to say it face to face. His cash flow was funny, and he was still tied up with his accountant. He couldn't go through with anything. "Sorry," he said. "Did you enjoy the drink? Tell Mack to pour you another, any kind you want, okay?"

"No thanks, I'll pass." I wasn't about to accept any conciliatory gesture, envisioning ringing the dude's neck after the time I'd spent and the promises he'd made. But I wasn't going to let my feelings show, staying cool as I walked back to my table and packed my gear. On my way out, I touched Wilbur on his shoulder, gave him a togetherness sign, and left.

The next day, I was still perturbed. Between losing the deal for the remotes, and not wanting to work Saturday, I thought of canceling, off and on, right up to the hour. I had personal things to do, no time to go fishing for uncertain hits. Yet, something deep inside kept pushing me, as if I was destined to go.

The insurance company's office was well lit, neat and tidy. Two young ladies strutted from desk to desk, shooting furtive glances my way and giggling. I could hear male voices rumbling from the next room. In minutes, a tall white man appeared at the entrance and stepped up to me.

"I'm Donald Lacey, WDDD general sales manager. I've been intending to get in touch with you to talk business. Can we get together sometime soon?"

WDDD was our main competition, but I handed him my card, "I'm sure we can make some kind of arrangement."

As Lacey turned to leave, he warned me, just above a whisper, "Lee's a hard nut to crack."

With Lacey gone, I sat listening to Lee's voice from the next office talking loudly on the phone like my grandmother who could never quite understand how someone miles away, on the other end, could hear her in her normal tone. I thought about this man who Wilbur called his partner, wondering if his arrogance that Wilbur had mentioned would require him to keep me waiting. If so, no sweat; to my surprise this operation looked like it would be a welcome addition to the auto risk insurance business I'd all but monopolized. I smiled to myself as I thought about his name, Robert E. Lee – now ain't that some shit for a spook to tag on his son.

Suddenly I heard the phone slam down, and saw the two young ladies scamper back to their desks and become ostentatiously busy. I figured Mr. Lee was about to appear.

"Welcome! Welcome!" Mr. Lee greeted me flamboyantly, both hands extended. He told the ladies I was the salesman from the "Senator's station" (at the time our listeners often identified The Tower by names of on-air personalities). But quickly, he turned off his smile and confronted me, "Did Mr. Parker tell you I called the station Thursday to talk with you? I talked to someone there, and told him why I was calling you, but he insisted on meeting with me Monday, himself. Is that the way you all work at your place?"

"No sir, not if you called for a particular person. They should have taken a message for me. But there was nothing..."

"From what Parker told me about you, I figured as much. That's why I'm squeezing you in now. C'mon." He swaggered towards his office, gesturing for me to follow, as he kept talking, "Would you care for coffee? Tea? I'll have one of the girls bring you whatever you want."

A picture of Dr. Martin Luther King hung above his desk. Mr. Lee sat tall, resting his head back in the palms of his hands. So self-assured he seemed cocky, he informed me he was twenty-nine and had a baby face, but don't let it fool you. Lee said he came up from Alabama and started this business two years ago, though people claimed he'd never make it. I could see he wasn't doing too badly.

Lee stared into my eyes and boasted, "I got six girls working out there, three salesmen in the street, a sales manager whose office is on that side of me, and a partner whose office is on the other side of me. I have five phone lines, which can be extended to nine. Plus, I have options on three more units in this complex. In other words, I'm prepared to handle any amount of business that comes my way, right? Now, what I want to know from you is, how much business can your station generate for me?"

He was precise, and full of himself, and I sensed he was used to getting what he wanted. I realized I'd have to be as assertive, and as specific, as he was.

I answered candidly that we couldn't generate any business for him; only inquiries, and the number would depend on his total program. First we'd determine a budget, how many spots to run, on which shows and what time of day. We'd discuss the approach, hard or soft sell, and then put together the right type of copy. I told him I needed to know more about his business and how closely we'd work. I asked him straight out where he wanted to go in his business and how soon he wished to get there. I wanted Lee to get to know me, and to talk in depth about what the station could offer.

Meanwhile, the phone was ringing, as I pressed on. Lee took a call, then another, and each time I picked up my thread, explaining the pluses and minuses of my station and the competitor. Then came another phone call. I was undaunted and returned to talking about each jock and the importance of each time slot.

All along, I wondered why Lee was accepting the calls. Was it to impress me more with his importance? If so, he'd already overplayed that. Or was it a ruse to disrupt and confuse my pitch, making me "easy pickin's" to be manhandled at his pleasure. Even so, I managed to restrain my annoyance while Lee relished his rude phone manners, all the while entertaining me with winks and gestures that expressed "I got these dudes in my hip pocket, baby."

One thing impressed me about Lee: he had an uncanny ability to resume our dialogue at the exact point of the interruption, never hesitating, never faltering. Probably he was comparing me to Lacey, and gradually I noticed him straightening in his seat, as if raising his antenna. As his attention grew, I saw he was finally coming down to earth. When Lee abruptly told his secretary to hold his calls, I knew I was in command.

"Did I hear you say the best time to advertise would be morning or afternoon drive-time?" Lee asked.

"It depends on your budget. If you can afford a few spots in housewife-time—9:00 a.m. to 3:00 p.m. – I'd recommend placing some there. As you know, in our market, many women work and make the final decision on the household budget. On the other hand, if your advertising budget is small, I'd suggest we spend it in drive-time only, where we'll have our maximum audience."

Lee wanted information on his competition – if they were advertising, how many spots they ran, what results they were getting. I gave him the information that was public; but, as for their results, I told Lee I didn't know.

"You don't know, or you won't say?"

"Both. First, I'm not privileged to that information. And, second, if I were, I wouldn't share it. You can understand that, of course. The same would apply to your business. It would be strictly between you and me. But I'll say this: your competition has been advertising with me for some time. That leads me to believe they're satisfied."

"Fine. But you can't give me any estimate of inquiries without knowing my budget."

I told him that was right, but I observed his finger fluttering on his lower lip. He needed something to grab onto, maybe something to share with his partner, or for his own assurance. But what? What would satisfy him without stepping beyond the bounds of truth? Then it came to me. I'd have to be tactful, because the information I wanted was guarded by most businesses. I needed their weekly financial reports. To my surprise, Lee handed them over immediately.

Studying the forms, I said, "This office averages about sixty inquiries and closes on about fifteen or twenty percent, right? Your average weekly cost for your salesmen is about one thousand dollars. And your salesmen bring in about sixty policies per week. Including your call-ins, your office averages about seventy-five policies per week, right? Now, by your own figures, I can take an amount of money equal to one-third of the dollars paid your salesmen and possibly produce at least seven times your weekly inquiries. That would mean more than four hundred compared to the sixty you're getting. Now, if we used your present closing ratio of twenty percent, you should close on eighty policies just from your advertising alone. Mr. Lee, look at that figure," I said, handing over my notepad. "That figure alone is more than what your entire office produces right now, isn't it?"

I sat back, feeling my full-court press had scored, knowing I'd performed well even though my spirits hadn't been up to speed. Even more important, I was satisfied I hadn't presented him with false hope; from my experience, I was well within the ballpark. When I saw Lee's eyes light up, I knew I'd cracked the nut. Still, I stayed cool, biding my time while Lee's eyes glazed as if counting up the dollars of potential business.

He asked, "How should we proceed?"

"I suggest we go slowly to monitor the response step by step. A couple of spots daily in morning-drive, and three in the afternoon-drive should do it for now."

"If this works out," Lee proclaimed, "it'll be only the beginning. How soon can we start?"

"I can have copies ready for your approval, Monday morning. If approved, we can start that afternoon."

"Fine." Mr. Lee said.

But before we were done, he motioned for me to hold on, while he fumbled through some notes. "Who's Karl Kruger?"

"He's a salesman at the station."

"He's the one I'd spoken with. Tell him not to come Monday. I won't be in. ... That reminds me, call me at this number to read me the copy on Monday." Lee handed me a slip of paper with an out-of-town number on it.

I felt like a little boy all over again, no troubles, no woes. My disappointment over the failed remotes deal last night with Randolph faded into the past as I motored west on 7 Mile Road. I'd let Lee think I'd tell Karl not to show up on Monday, but I had no intention to tell Karl anything. All along, I'd suspected he was the culprit from my past experience with him and from hearing other salesmen grumble that Karl was trying to steal their accounts too. I laughed, getting a big kick out of turning the table on Karl. My only wish was to be a speck on the wall, come Monday, so I could observe the sucker's face.

The sun had popped out, and its brightness along with the hit invigorated me so much I was boogeying in my seat to the music on my station, allowing my euphoria to burst out. Never mind that the people in passing rides might think I was crazy. Who were they anyway? Why should I even care? I'd made my first big kill and I liked the taste of blood.

CHAPTER THREE

On Monday, when the contract crossed Bonner's desk, he looked it over, then handed it to Karl, who sat waiting, his anxiety rising. Bonner asked him if this was from the person he'd mentioned. Through the plasterboard wall that separated Bonner's office from his secretary, she could hear Karl throw the contract across the desk, jump up, and explode.

Karl told Bonner he'd talked to Lee on Thursday and set up an appointment, but when he got there the bastard wasn't even in. Then some girl in that damn place told him that I had come in Saturday, left with a contract, and the ads would start this afternoon.

"Calm down," Bonner said. "Others might hear you."

Karl didn't care who heard him. He told Bonner that he was so damn numb when he found out what had happened, someone could've hit him over the head with a hammer and he wouldn't have felt a thing. It should've been his account. It's a good piece of business. And if I get it, they'd never get rid of me.

Actually, Bonner was no longer trying to get rid of me, since I turned out not to be the flash in the pan that Karl hoped. I was holding my own, and that was helping Bonner come closer to meeting his yearly sales projection. And now that the announcers' strike was over, he didn't need any more problems anytime soon.

Bonner said, "This isn't like those other accounts I've turned over to you."

Karl claimed it had to be his because I didn't have the ability to get it on my own. Bonner didn't know how to answer, so he came up with a solution – he called Mr. Lee's office directly. Of course, Lee was out for the day.

"Now what?" Karl was champing at the bit.

Bonner wouldn't sign the contract until he found out what was going on, but he didn't want trouble in the office. So Bonner took Karl downstairs for coffee to cool him off.

Meanwhile, Rose, Bonner's secretary, put a message in my box to get in touch with her immediately. Having been nurtured in a household of females, I'd been taught how to treat them, and had an especially good rapport with Rose. I'd taken her out to the new Playboy Club on Jefferson, and taught her the twist, the new dance craze. I genuinely liked taking all the ladies out to lunch on special occasions; besides, it kept them in my corner.

The minute I returned to the office, I picked up her message, and she repeated every word she'd heard. She asked me not to let on that she'd told me. I nodded and smiled as I returned to my desk. I'd been waiting for this moment, anticipating throwing cold water on Karl's arrogant greed. I figured that Bonner would favor Karl. But this time I was prepared. It wasn't long before Bonner summoned me.

As I walked in, Bonner was standing behind his desk, fingering the shaggy cord of the Venetian blind that covered the large, dirty window. He turned and picked up the contract, and waved it towards me.

"I have a problem with this," he began. He explained what Karl told him, and finally took his seat. "I want to know two things. First, is Karl's story correct? And second, if not, how did you come by the contract?"

I laid out the facts. But Bonner refused to believe that Karl would intercept a call from my client and then make an appointment to see him instead of leaving a message for me.

"Believe it," I stated.

Bonner paused. He had to consider how all of this might play if the skirmish ever reached The Buhl. No doubt, he'd assured Karl he'd get what he wanted. But The Buhl was pressuring Bonner for more business, and this contract was a big piece of business, big enough to force me to take my grievance to The Buhl if Karl got credit for it. No, Bonner had to handle this situation with finesse. He thought he had the right approach.

"I have your last two weekly reports here," Bonner said to me. "I couldn't find any mention of this account in them."

I told him he would have to go back three or four weeks and that it was under Wilbur Parker, Mr. Lee's partner.

"I don't keep my copies that far back," Bonner said. "Do you have yours?"

"Yes, at home in my files."

"That doesn't help our present situation, does it?"

"No. But then, did Karl show you his?" I challenged, knowing Karl couldn't have.

"No, but I have his word."

"Oh, we're back to Karl's word again," I smiled, well aware of the complicity.

Bonner got my point, and averted his eyes, setting aside the papers on his desk. "I don't know what you mean by that. I'm going to hold up this ad until I get more evidence."

"It's running now."

"I can stop it," Bonner asserted stubbornly, as he reached for his phone.

I was prepared for this. When I'd called Lee earlier to read him the copy, I warned him he might get a call from Bonner, and why. Now the time had come to show my hand. I reached in my breast pocket and extracted the out-of-town number Lee had given me.

"Why don't we just call Mr. Lee? May I try?" I reached for the phone, adding, "I'm sure you agree it's only right to talk to him before putting a hold on his schedule."

Confident that Lee was still out of his office, so I'd get nowhere with the call, Bonner put the phone in my hand. I dialed the out-of-town number, and gave the phone back to Bonner.

"Hello," Bonner said, stunned. "Is this Mr. Lee?" he stammered.

The call took only a few minutes, during which Bonner apologized for intruding on Lee's day, before he hung up, red-faced.

"Well, did that resolve your question?" I asked.

"I just wanted to make sure," Bonner, muttered, "I don't need any hassles."

"There were none to be had," I answered pointedly.

Bonner shook his head, as if he was dazed, "Who is he? I never heard of him?"

"With due respect, sir, I'm not surprised. I suppose there are many people in my market you wouldn't know anything about. Lee's a friend of mine who has a growing company, and who recognizes our market's potential and has the guts to go after it."

Bonner kept struggling to wrap his mind around the situation. "Well, he's spending a pretty penny. Is he financially responsible? Watch the collections closely."

I gave him no response. Finally, realizing he had no way out, he switched to flattering me. I'd learned that was Bonner's way of cultivating the trust of those from whom he wanted something in return. I listened to the praise, unsure how much might have been genuine, and how much was luring me off-guard so he could stab me in the back. Regardless, I wasn't taking any chances. I had to keep my cool and understand that after all was said and done, my only safeguard lay in what I could accomplish on the job.

I played by the rules, checking in every day, and meeting with Bonner biweekly to detail my progress report and my monthly business forecast. I was making real commissions now. I had a handle on Bonner's quirks and office politics. In the four years I'd given myself, I was on the way to the yellow brick road to success. But I was still the low man on the totem pole, and a long way from where I intended, so I needed to keep my mask on.

Two months later, in August 1963, Dr. King gave his memorable "I Have a Dream" speech at the March on Washington, espousing the brotherhood of all people. His call for justice inspired an emotional and philosophic unanimity from listeners of every background, who stood shoulder to shoulder in solidarity for civil rights. Clearly, Dr. King had touched the conscience of many Americans, and that helped build the clamor for passage of the Civil Rights Bill. But for long-dispossessed Negroes, the event meant far more: they witnessed the power that flowed from our numbers, our faith, and the strength of our survival. I drew courage from it, myself, and started to think about hitting the big agencies for new business.

In all of television, I remembered one short-run laundry soap commercial in which a sister was spotted in a Laundromat. My market was invisible in advertiser's commercial packages, and yet the advertising industry seemed to run the media. I realized the big agencies were my ticket, and I'd have to learn how they worked.

So I began attending the open weekly luncheons of the Adcraft Club of Detroit that featured prominent speakers from business, government, and other sectors. Adcraft was the largest advertising association in America, and included many of the top-level executives of agencies, media, and graphics arts firms, among its all-male membership. Each time I went, I psyched myself up to endure being the only person of color present. As a pioneer, I had to bear it if I was going to understand the minds of these men, some of whom had helped establish the industry, men who had the expertise that I wanted.

Later, I joined, and in time, after mingling with more and more agency people at the luncheons, my fear of the big agencies dissipated somewhat. Now I was ready to approach them. The ones with automotive clients that the sales staff never tapped became my targets. Many had offices within two miles of The Tower – J. Walter Thompson, Kenyon Eckhardt, McCann-Erickson, D.P. Brothers, Leo Burnett, BBD&O, and Young & Rubican. Intently, I put my presentation together, revved my motor, and set out in high gear on my quest, more bullish than ever, determined to crack open doors, confident of taking on whomever.

On my first approach, I didn't burden the buyers with lengthy statistics on my market. Instead, I gave them its basics, for example that the market would be easy to access because the people lived in concentrated areas and were loyal to brand name products, which served them. I told them Detroit was the nation's fourth largest Negro market, comprising nearly thirty percent of the city's population, and that the market was growing because of our higher birth rate and the continuous influx of Negroes to the city, in contrast to whites who were moving out. I projected the market would reach 40% of the city within the next five years. I apprised them the population was younger than whites, on average, and the younger generation tended to be more educated, which means they'd earn a higher income in the future. I told them the market's median income of $4,543, earned mainly from working in heavy industry, was much higher than the national Negro median of $3,399, thereby making the Detroit market a major consumer testing area.

For all the information, the buyers responded only politely. Hardly a question was raised in my allotted time. Such a tremendous gap seemed to persist between the facts I was stating – the aspirations, the priorities, the potentials of this market – and the world these agencies knew that it was almost as if I was talking in a foreign tongue in the absence of an interpreter whose credibility would have gained our mutual respect. I found myself in uncharted territory, caught up in a different world where Negroes were invisible; we simply didn't exist. They didn't dismiss me directly—"Don't call me, I'll call you" was not my impression. On the other hand, neither was "Keep in touch."

I decided to pursue those few buyers who'd shown some interest and put aside all the ones I'd have to spend a long time educating. Some day I'd return, but now I couldn't afford any dead weight. I whipped off letters thanking all of them, and thought about the whole hunt as a blessing in disguise. Now I knew for sure what the big agencies looked like, and to that degree, I'd penetrated the world of the image-makers, the world of the mass opinion-manipulators. And I'd found it, in the main, not ready.

By 1964, as a result of great efforts by Dr. King and other leaders after the assassination of President John Kennedy, President

Johnson signed the Civil Rights Bill into law. It prohibited discrimination in the workplace and in public, but throughout the country, the law did little to change people's attitudes. As the holiday season approached, I felt the Struggle continuing unabated.

Around this time, I'd gone to another of the corporate gatherings – a buyer named Blake Roper at Campbell Ewald hosted this one. Media reps who serviced the metro area had formed a line to shake Blake's hand at the end of the meeting, and to make their last minute bid on a Chevy buy. Next to me in line stood Donald Lacey, the General Sales Manager at Negro-owned WDDD, who had tried for Mr. Lee's contract that I won. He asked if I thought our stations had a chance of making this buy.

I told him honestly that I'd been to Kenyon-Eckhart on Mercury, to Young & Rubican on Dodge, to J. Walter Thompson on Ford, and to MacManus, John and Adam on Cadillac – all to end up empty-handed. I'd sent Blake materials and he'd shown some interest, so I was keeping an open mind about him. Actually, Blake was the only truly encouraging buyer, and I couldn't help being hopeful. Maybe Lacey felt that.

"You're next," he whispered. "Wait for me – I want to talk when you're done."

As I shook Blake's hand, I asked if he'd gotten a chance to go over my market demographics that I'd left with Carol, his secretary. Blake was honest. He'd received everything, and it all looked very good. But he hadn't been able to arrange the meeting between me and the media planner and the account executive. Then he pulled me aside and whispered candidly that the people over him were guarding the status quo. Nobody wanted to be the first to try something different for fear of failure. All they wanted was to keep their keys to the executive johns and their offices with windows.

"So you're not on this buy," Blake said, "I'm sorry. But in the meantime, I'll keep trying. Stay in touch. Maybe soon, instead of our usual three martini lunch, we can brown-bag-it while shooting pool, downstairs."

I waited for Lacey outside the room, making small talk with

Carol. I'd been through this kind of thing too many times before to let it show that I was disappointed, or to have really expected anything else. Finally Lacey came out. "What's on your mind?" I asked.

"Let's get a drink," he responded, heading for the door, "I'm buying."

We settled in the small café downstairs, waiting on our drinks. Lacey was a big man, about six-four, square-jawed with a full head of black hair slicked like armor-plating, his brown eyes were intensely hardened like a gunfighter just before the moment of reckoning. I could see something was bothering him. When the drinks arrived, I lit up a smoke and broke the impasse, "What's the problem?"

Lacey said he needed to talk to someone. He'd come from WYMK in Chicago and hadn't met too many people in Detroit he could talk to, but he'd heard nice things about me. Still, he'd been reluctant to come to me because we're competitors. Opening up, he complained that he got no cooperation from the people at his station, especially the ownership. The prominent upper class Negroes who owned WDDD weren't pleased with one of their biggest on-air personalities, who called herself "Her Majesty," yet her show was where Lacey's salesmen could place a lot of business. The owners said she's "country," and she talks down to her people, especially colored men. Lacey didn't know what to do.

I'd been in this situation before – a white man asking for my help interpreting black-on-black attitudes – and there was only so far I was going to go, especially since Lacey was the competition, after all. But I had to agree that I'd listened to Her Majesty, and though she came across as overbearing, I believed she'd be an asset to any station. Secretly, I was thinking I'd like to have her on WTOP, and if she wasn't happy elsewhere… But I didn't go down that road, at least not yet. I changed the subject to the agencies we were both pitching.

Lacey was doing even worse than I was. "I'd like to pick your brains," he confided honestly. "How do you go about selling the agencies? I lost out to you lots of times. I read *Advertising Age*, *Media Scope*, *Sponsor*, and all the other trades to find out what's happening, but I can't get to first base with most agencies, and I don't know why. This market is even better than Chicago. What are you doing?"

I let him have a peek into my style, knowing it was grounded in my understanding of the community, which he'd never be able to touch, simply because it's not where he came from. I told Lacey that in my second round with buyers, like Blake, I realized the relationship would have to be a two-way street, symbiotic, not parasitic. I gave them presentations beyond what they were used to.

I talk to them about the importance of Negro music in good times and bad—how songs, going back to the plantation work songs of my forefathers, became a main stem of Negro culture, how music had linked slaves of different tribal tongues when other forms of communication were prohibited, giving them a group identity in an otherwise insidious system of depressed isolation. I talk to the buyers about how drums not only thumped out the beat for dancing feet but also conveyed messages from plantation to plantation. And then I lead them to understand how gospels, blues, rhythm'n'blues and jazz all grew out of the rich spirituals, and they all formed a cultural linkage for Negroes from slavery up to now. Music has always healed the Negro soul and nurtured our spiritual life. Finally, to put everything in perspective, I tell the buyers that aside from playing records at home, the only medium where my market can experience this musical linkage is on the few Negro-oriented radio stations. That's a tremendous potential power to showcase their products.

Lacey listened hard, though his body language was becoming defensive. After all, the African-American cultural roots weren't in his interest. "That's all fine," Lacey finally responded, "but what do you say when buyers tell you there'll be no such thing as Negro radio because in ten or fifteen years the general stations will consume it?"

"I would say bullshit! How can general radio consume Negro radio when most stations refuse to give airplay to any of Motown's biggest hits, because they're too scared the music will alienate their white audience? What a laugh! They're playing rock'n'roll, aren't they? What's rock'n'roll if not white man's attempt at a version of rhythm'n'blues?

"Lacey, if you know the history of radio, you should know, as well as I do, that the record industry has always pressed white cover versions of Negro artists' songs so they could be played on general radio and make them money. Take Little Richard's 'Tutti-Frutti.' Pat Boone recorded it for general radio, and it became the number one seller. In the '30s and '40s, they took jazz and changed it to swing, then called Benny Goodman 'king of swing.' In the fifties, after everyone had TVs, general radio was pressed to find new ways to enlarge its audience and still not play rhythm'n'blues. You remember what happened—Alan Freed and general radio tried to steal rhythm'n'blues by putting a white face on it and tagging it rock'n'roll. Then they crowned Elvis as its king, as if a new creation was born just so it could be played on general radio stations. Hardly anybody in the general market is even aware of James Brown or Aretha Franklin, are they?"

I knew I was going on, maybe too much, but at that moment I didn't care. Lacey needed to hear this, and after today's disappointment, maybe I needed to let it all hang out. So I finished, "No! General radio is racist. It'll never consume Negro radio in a hundred years. I'd take it as a personal insult if anyone says otherwise because that implies my musical taste can be easily manipulated to the general market's thinking."

I took a breath and sat back. Lacey raised his glass. "I can't argue with you. That's the best answer I ever heard. I wish I could use it. But who'd believe that, coming from me. If I could only get my salesmen to be more like you..." He thought, then took the leap, "Look, are you satisfied at your station? I sure could use a good man like you."

"While there are things at The Tower I don't like, I know the score," I answered. "No one there has the knowledge I have, or my track record. So, in a sense, I'm my own boss. I like it that way. Besides, I have too much on the books to leave."

"Don't worry about leaving your accounts. I can make up everything you'd lose."

"How so?"

"I'll take them from the other salesmen. They're not doing much with them anyway."

I looked at my watch—time to move on. "Sorry, man, that's a no-no. That way of dealing reminds me of what I don't like at my place. But let me give you some advice: At WDDD you can't afford the luxury of not understanding the Negro market's soul. The real pulse can't be acquired by reading the trade magazines – they're just beginning to look at us from afar. As for the daily papers, aside from articles about the Civil Rights Movement, a small sports feature, and lots of crime, of course, they have no desire to learn or communicate what our market cares about."

I told him, "get out from behind your desk and into the community, or you can't front yourself off to others as knowing what would sell to this market. As General Sales Manager, no matter your color, if you did your homework, then you could talk with anyone with some authority. But just using the tired approach that WDDD is one of the first Negro-owned stations won't cut it anymore. It doesn't sell."

A wounded Lacey slumped at the table, drained of pride and sureness. I had intended to touch a nerve, but not to cut so deeply. Still, the damage was done, and there was no way to get around it. I stood, shook Lacey's hand, thanked him for the drink, and wished him a happy holiday season.

Of course, we were destined to meet again, and when we did, Lacey would remember this day.

CHAPTER FOUR

Always in a rush, I was running late to join the sales staff at its annual Christmas luncheon. Actually, I wasn't planning to attend at all until I found out that Mr. Beck, the head of The Buhl, had directed Ed Butler (The Buhl's Vice President and Controller) to attend for the first time. Butler, I knew, was Bonner's nemesis, so I wanted to size him up and observe the interaction between the two.

From the moment I entered Cliff Bells, a popular business restaurant a couple of blocks from The Tower, the festive atmosphere grabbed me. Heading towards the staff's table, I saw Butler, an unimpressive, small man wearing large horn-rim glasses that seemed too heavy to rest on his nose. Well aware that Butler had been with Mr. Beck since day one, and was second in command, I watched Butler carefully, while pretending to listen to Henry's tripe talk and Karl's corny jokes.

Rumors had been floating that Bonner was on the verge of getting fired, so he appeared stiffer than usual and kind of antsy. Clearly, he detested Butler's presence, and probably suspected Butler was judging him, preparing to report a heap of negative bull back to Mr. Beck. Bonner was determined not to be his patsy, wasn't about to give him ammunition, so he ate his lunch on guard, contributing little to the conversation, and left shortly after lunch, unable to take the strain of Butler's company any longer.

In contrast, Butler proposed toast after toast – to Henry's vacation, to the season, to any other excuse that came to mind. After a few more rounds, he was giddy. Slurring his speech, his subject turned to women, making lewd remarks while the others egged him on. He prompted me to join in, but I found the condescending comments about women juvenile and disgusting, and refused to get involved. I wondered if this was the true character of a man in his position, and if not, what point was he endeavoring to make? I watched and said nothing.

Finally, Butler turned to me, leery of my silence, and asked if I was bored with their company. He'd heard from the others that I was always involved with the good lookers. "Why not introduce me to some of your lady friends?" Butler prodded. "Better yet, why not take us to one of those nightspots you've been advertising? This is the season to be jolly. You know what I mean?" he chuckled along with the others.

So that was it – Butler simply wanted some black meat. But how could he be so bold-faced, knowing so little about me, and especially on our very first meeting? Did Butler figure I was gullible and would yield to the pressure of his position? Or did he figure I was moonlighting as a procurer of women? While I did know a few scarlet ladies in the past, a pimp I certainly was not. The very idea was an insult; I'd sworn I'd never be a part of that. Nevertheless, I considered the situation, and became intrigued: How could I use this chance meeting to my advantage? I'd already gained more insight into station politics, and the thought of getting nearer to The Buhl and undermining someone in authority there was very seductive.

I answered him, "If you're talking about getting someone in bed, I might be able to hook you up with a ten-dollar whore. Other than that, I couldn't connect you to anyone. And you'd have to follow my lead. Can you handle that?"

Two salesmen shied away. Butler was ready. Karl and Henry just wanted to tag along. So, each in his own ride, followed me uptown.

The club uptown was familiar to me but far outside the world of these men. Guiding them through the black'n'tan clamor in the smoke-filled room, I situated them at the bar. I introduced them to Doug, the bartender, and as he took our orders, an attractive young lady slithered up behind me and kissed me on the neck. Surprised, I turned and recognized an old high school girlfriend I hadn't seen for years. We hugged and chatted a while. As she was about to walk away, she handed me her card and asked me to call her.

No sooner was she gone than Butler made an off-color remark. I wasn't going to take that – especially not on my home ground. I put aside my mask and let him know he'd offended me.

"I meant no harm," Butler said. "She struck me, and I just wondered why you didn't introduce me."

"Her name escaped me," I lied.

"I didn't need to know her name. I just wanted to meet her. You know what I mean," Butler insisted with a silly grin.

Sure I knew what he meant. I told him my friend was not about to lay down with him, so he'd better forget about her. I repeated the type I could get him, and I'd let him know when I spotted one. But that didn't register with Butler, who continued to pester me like a kid nagging his parent for a lollypop. It got to the point that I had to remind him that I was in charge, and to cool it.

As the evening went on, the crowd thickened and a quartet assembled on stage, and Butler was still hot to trot. I was really trying to accommodate him, but I couldn't spot any whores. I'd thought for sure they'd show up when the after-work crowd arrived. Not one. But searching the other side of the bar, I spied Fast Eddie; a pimp with whom I'd forged a friendship when I was young and hanging out on the streets. I excused myself, ploughed through the crowd, and pulled Fast Eddie aside.

"Muh man, where're all the ladies?" I asked.

"This is the holiday season, muh man. They're busy. At least mine are. What's up Strict Business? Since you made that move downtown, it's been awhile. Now don't tell me you're on the prowl."

I explained, and Eddie sympathized, "Ruby's right across the street. Did you check her out?"

"Nah, man. I lost track of her after she left Orchestra Place."

"Under the circumstances, c'mon and renew your acquaintance."

I told my party I'd be right back and left with Fast Eddie. We walked up the squeaky, dimly lit stairway to the second floor landing then made our way to Ruby's at the end of the hall. Fast Eddie knocked. In seconds the door opened. A man led us into the dining room. I greeted Ruby with a big hug, talked a little, and then told her why I was here. She pointed to the sofa where two hungry-looking "bears" sat licking their chops for a taste of honey.

"What do you think?" she asked me, indicating her available girls.

"Would you take them on?" I whispered sarcastically to Fast Eddie.

"Nah, baby, but who knows, maybe your man will if all he wants is a piece of black meat."

"That's a good point. Besides, this'll be his last chance because I'm tired of hangin' with this shit on my back."

I returned to the bar and told Butler what I could offer. He went back to Ruby's with me, and she gave him the choice of the two girls. He wanted both. So I told Ruby where she could find me, got her assurance that Butler would be in good hands, and I split.

Back at the bar, I asked Fast Eddie if he still used the "Silencer?" Fast Eddie smiled, "You remember that after all these years?"

"Why not? You were always bragging about it."

Eddie pulled a small tape recorder from his pocket. "Why did you ask?"

"I was thinking about using one for insurance, if you got a spare tape. I'll straighten you."

"No need, muh man. Take this. It's loaded. I got more in my ride."

About an hour later, I got a phone call at the bar to go back to Ruby's. Butler was complaining that the house had stolen his money.

"But that's not so," Ruby explained when I walked in. "He was never satisfied. He insisted on more and more. And, of course, that means he had to shell out more bread."

"What room is he in?" I asked.

"The first to your left."

I turned on the Silencer, whispered into it the date and time, then knocked and entered. The girls had left Butler sprawled out naked on the bed, clenching some money in his fist.

"What's the problem?" I asked.

Butler opened his fist. "See, they took my money."

He'd had about eighty-three dollars, and twenty-six were left. I reminded him he'd been there with the two girls for over an hour. And didn't he buy drinks, and have the girls lay with him more than once? Butler nodded.

"Then that's it. What more do you want? Put your clothes on. Let's get out of here," I said.

Butler wasn't ready to leave. He had some money left and wanted to stay. I told him if that's what he wanted, then he was on his own. I was no longer going to wet-nurse him. I left the room, shut off the Silencer, and returned to Ruby. She promised not to serve Butler any more liquor and to see he got to his ride safely. Then I went back to the club.

Karl and Henry had left, which freed me to move around. I came upon Fast Eddie.

"How'd it go?" Fast Eddie asked.

"No problem – thanks," I answered to avoid getting into too much about Butler. When one of Fast Eddie's girls caught up with him, I glanced around to spot my high school sweetheart, but she had left. So I settled quietly at the bar, sipped a couple of martinis, listened to a set, and vowed never again.

Early the next morning, Saturday, hung-over, I was wakened by a call. It was Butler, asking me to forget what had happened, and if anyone asked about Friday, insist that everyone went his own way after lunch. Butler gave me his private number and said to call him as soon as I got in on Monday – he'd explain then. It was a strange, urgent call; the first time Butler had ever called me, at home or otherwise. Something must have happened after I left. What more might have gone down?

Monday. I was taking a shortcut across Grand Circus Park, and stopped to flip a half-buck to a panhandler near The Tower, when I heard a voice calling my name. I turned and saw Karl racing up to stop me short of entering the building. Breathless, Karl said all hell had broken out! Butler could be in serious trouble with Mr. Beck. And Bonner, knowing how strict Beck was about his employees, was trying to find out anything he might use against Butler. Karl cautioned me to play dumb.

Sure enough, in The Tower's lobby, Beverly, the switchboard operator, said Bonner was waiting to see me. Indeed, I also found a message from Bonner in my box to see him ASAP. I wondered what could have happened to involve me so desperately. Did Butler mess up?

I stopped at my office first and called Butler's private line to tell him I'd get back to him after I'd met with Bonner. If the meeting turned out to be about last Friday, I'd keep the evening confidential, as I'd promised.

Sitting behind his desk Bonner greeted me with a broad smile and said make myself comfortable. Evidently, Bonner figured that with my help he could position himself to strike back at Butler by discrediting him, and take the heat off himself. By now, I could see through Bonner's pretenses, and knew his approach would be to catch me off guard. I relished the thought of confounding his intentions, and was determined that no matter what Bonner asked, my replies would be short and to the point – no more.

"Are you all set for the holidays?" Bonner began.

"I sent out some cards to clients and bought a few gifts. I might say that I am."

"I got a few things to do, myself," Bonner smiled. "Mostly, I leave the biggest part of the holidays for my wife to handle. How's business?" Bonner switched gears, though he was still smiling.

"All my contracts cross your desk, and you see all of my daily reports," I responded, matter-of-fact.

A moment passed in silence. Bonner hadn't expected me to be quite so blunt. Maybe he'd caught on that I was aware of what he was contriving. He'd have to do a better job if he didn't want it to appear that he was after Butler's scalp.

"You're right about that, my boy," Bonner chuckled. "It was a moot question, but there are times when I'm not thinking right. Take last Friday—I could've stayed at the luncheon longer. I guess I left too early to be part of the real celebration. What happened after I left?"

To Bonner's credit, the way he changed the subject to his real interest was pretty smooth but not smooth enough for me. I informed him I'd left the others. Whether they stayed there or went elsewhere, I couldn't say.

"Are you sure you're not protecting someone?"

"Who would I protect? And why would I lie about going or staying?"

Bonner backtracked – he didn't mean to infer that I was lying. He just thought I was with the others and knew what happened to Ed Butler. But Bonner implied that if it ever came out to be what he heard, Mr. Beck wouldn't look kindly on the others or me.

"At the moment," I said, "I don't know what you're talking about. Why don't you just tell me what you heard?"

Bonner's smile was gone now. He said he'd heard that it didn't end at lunch and that I'd taken the others somewhere else, and I took Ed Butler off to hunt for a prostitute.

"That's not true. I'd like to know who's responsible for that lie."

"I can't say. I promised to keep his name out of it. But he's quite sure you knew everything. Plus, he said that after Ed left with you, he never saw him again."

Now I knew who the culprit was, but I decided to play along. "You're telling me that someone has accused me and I have no way of confronting him? You know that's not right!"

"I don't look at it that way. I thought if anybody knew and would tell me the truth it would be you, that's all."

"Are you at liberty to tell me everything you know?" I probed.

Bonner revealed that Butler was found the next morning in his driveway, drunk in his car. His clothes were disheveled, he'd lost his money, and his wife needed help to carry him into the house.

Relieved that Butler had gotten home safely, and that what had happened occurred at his house and not at Ruby's, I asked, "Where did he say he'd been?"

"He couldn't remember. His wife called Mr. Beck Saturday to find out. Then Mr. Beck called me. He's hopping mad, and he's been on my back ever since. You're the only one I can trust. I wanted to let you know the rumors, and to protect you from Mr. Beck."

Now knowing the big picture, and all too aware of Bonner's way of conning people, I replied with a degree of humility, "I'm sorry, sir. You can be assured that I would if I could."

That was a blow to Bonner. He'd thought he had an advantage with me. No doubt he believed I hadn't been straight up with him, and that he'd come up against what he thought was my streak of stubbornness. In any case, Bonner had to resign himself that it would be futile to press me further.

"All right," Bonner said. "If you don't know what happened, you don't know."

I left enjoined by my conscience for telling a lie. It wasn't my bag, and it robbed me of the value of truth. But why should I let this bug me? The system was full of lies, and if I was going to stay abreast of the game and carry out my real purpose of getting close to the power, I had no choice but to play by their rules.

Anyway, I was satisfied on two accounts: One, I hadn't given Bonner any satisfaction. Two, Bonner had unwittingly named the person who squealed on us. But why did he do it? And why had the culprit approached me earlier? Was it an attempt to deflect suspicion that he was the traitor?

Later in the day, I met Butler at a coffee shop a few blocks away, and we compared notes. I'd first thought of not revealing the snitch's name. But after more consideration, I concluded that stirring up mistrust between the two might work to my advantage and shore up my screws on Butler in the process. So when asked if I had any idea who'd squealed to Bonner, I told him. But Butler had a difficult time believing me.

"It can only be him," I argued. "Besides you and me, only two others were there. Henry left the same night to go on vacation. That only leaves Karl, unless you think it was me, but I'd stand to lose the most if this all came out."

"But Karl's a close friend. Why would he do that?"

"I have no idea. But when I was a very young man, I learned to check my checkers, and to watch my watchers. Maybe the same needs to be said about some friends."

I left it there for Butler to mull over. Whether he believed me or not was no longer my concern. I knew Butler owed me, and psychologically would always be in my grasp, though where my actions would take me, I could only speculate.

Another year was about to begin. It was imperative for me to keep my character in the community intact and press on.

CHAPTER FIVE

In early '65, Malcolm X's assassination shook Negro communities across the country. Grief-stricken, few Negroes accepted the version put out in the papers that Black Muslims were responsible for his homicide. Rather, many suspected the government had played a significant role and the killing showed to what extreme it might go to eliminate the Negro leadership. Not everyone believed that, of course. The general media had distorted Malcolm's actual revolutionary, provocative messages, depicting him as simply negative, so for those who'd accepted what they were told, the slaying didn't matter.

But Malcolm had wakened the sleeping Black Giant, teaching him to know himself, believe in himself, have self-respect and take pride in him. Malcolm embodied what the Negro male wanted to be and guided him, and heartfelt memorial services were held in honor of his birthday all around Detroit.

As for me, Malcolm's death plunged me deep into memories of this great man whom I'd had the pleasure of meeting and hearing at the overcrowded Central United Church of Christ on Linwood Street. I spent two weeks alone paying tribute to him, replaying his album, "Malcolm Speaks to the Grassroots," withdrawn from my usual business pace to be present at venues eulogizing his name.

When I got back on track, my first stop was Lee's agency. With every desk occupied, even Lee was scurrying from one cabinet to another, pulling files to help the overworked girls. From the waiting area I watched the fit of energy. Eventually, I peeked behind a black canvas that was hung over the entrance to another unit and saw men busy painting the walls, preparing an expanded area. Lee spotted me and motioned me in. Squeezing between cabinets that lined the hallway, I settled into his office.

Over time, my relationship with Lee had mellowed. We'd learned to respect and trust each other, and Lee relied on my guidance. Hearing the clamor in the office, I felt proud, knowing I'd played an important role in getting the business to this point. Lee wanted to know if I'd looked over his proposals for new branch offices in densely populated areas, which had many businesses and heavy traffic, exactly as I'd recommended. "They're perfect spots," I assured him.

This was the time for him to grow because a bill pending in Lansing was due to pass requiring everyone to have insurance in order to get a license plate. Lee would be able to contract with more carriers and write as much business as he could get. "I got to be ready," Lee, said. "I want to get into phase two as soon as possible. What're my chances?"

I asked if he'd done what I'd suggested – filed an assumed name and set up the house-advertising agency to get that fifteen percent off the top. Lee had done as I'd said, but he doubted the station would be wiling to recognize his agency anyway. I assured him the station had no choice. The practice was perfectly legal, but, more than that, it was about the money. Lee would become the biggest spot advertiser by far in the station's history, and no one there would have the guts to reject his contract. In fact, I told him that with a contract that size I might be able to wiggle twenty or more free promote spots out of Bonner. I said don't count on it, but if an opening comes, take it and see what happens.

"Besides I already talked to Ed Butler about it," I confided, reminding Lee that Butler was my pigeon, as well as the station's accountant and VP.

We planned our approach and our objectives. We would meet with Bonner for his verification on our points and to get his signature on the contract to prevent any future discrepancies with him or anyone else. By now I was wise to the tricks they might try if every item wasn't spelled out and signed.

Two days later at The Buhl, Mr. Thornton W. Beck and Ed Butler were poring over financial statements for their yearly fiscal report. Mr. Beck, tall and ruggedly handsome, dominated his privately owned company. Once considered the black sheep in a lineage of wealth, he'd worked hard to overcome an early stigma of failure. Now married with two teenage sons, he'd succeeded and proved to be no fool.

Butler's extreme loyalty to Mr. Beck contrasted with his insidious way of subtly undermining those of lesser status. His underlings called him a pip-squeak in whispers, though they feared he was so untrustworthy he'd turn on his own mother if need be.

"You may have to cut back on buying Cat-TV—it's draining your overall radio profits. See," Butler said, pointing to the bottom line. "We're nearing red ink."

"Cat-TV will be a moneymaker in time, and now's the time to get as many licenses as I can. How's my Cleveland station doing? What's going on in Indiana? Is The Tower doing any better?" Mr. Beck probed anxiously.

Butler argued, "We got to do much better everywhere to keep up with the drainage, at least a ten or fifteen percent increase overall. Why not call a meeting of all management; give them a pep talk; tell them what you need. If they succeed, they'll get a car for a bonus. If they can't perform, they'll be fired or their overrides will be reduced."

Meanwhile, at The Tower, Bonner was awaiting a meeting with Lee, though he knew nothing about what Lee wanted. As for me, this was payback time – my payback to Bonner for stabbing me in the back. I'd learned from past experiences that it was too easy for

Bonner to refuse a wish or two of my clients in their absence, but in their presence, Bonner had difficulty turning anything down, especially if he was facing the clients cold. My plan was to keep Bonner off guard before compelling him to acquiesce to our plan.

Bonner's first jolt came when Lee stepped into his office, along with me. Bonner's military bearing faltered and his face flushed in spite of his efforts to smile and act cordial. He'd never asked about Lee's color; therefore, I'd never mentioned it. Because of Lee's name and his budget—which was equaled only by a few national accounts but certainly not by any local client on the station -- Bonner had assumed Lee was white.

After making the introduction, I shut up and sat back, as planned, confident that Bonner would try to seduce Lee with flattery. Sure enough, as always, Bonner spilled it out non-stop, ending with his offer of complete cooperation. His unctuous words used to lull Lee into a sense of well being had my stomach turning. Out of Bonner's view, I nudged Lee's foot with mine; knowing Lee would get my meaning.

It was show time – Lee's turn. Forewarned, he was not gullible. As planned, he started out slowly, acknowledging the astute, insightful observations I had shared to help his agency prosper. He then began spreading the butter, thick and heavy, on the station and on Bonner as well. His rhythmic cadence was reminiscent of a country preacher in sermon stirring up his flock, and then caressing their troubled souls with promises of everlasting life. It brought a clenched smile to my face and held Bonner enthralled with an ear-to-ear grin glued on his face. When Lee ended with, "I value your judgment, sir. Won't you please be my friend?" Bonner threw up his hands in glee, as if to say hallelujah, you can lean on me.

My nerves were tingling in want of comic relief. I looked to Lee to give him a solemn nod of approval. But seeing Lee sitting there so erect, so straight-faced, so sanctimonious, an even bigger hypocrite than Bonner, caused me to call on all my will power to overcome my intense urge to giggle openly. I needed to get my mind back on track to the business at hand.

"Is there such a thing as an advertiser saturating a definite time?" Lee asked Bonner with pure innocence. "If so, what would be the requirements? I'm curious."

"There is such a thing, my friend. It's called exclusivity. But it's very costly," Bonner smiled benevolently then went on to explain.

"An advertiser can get a guarantee of exclusivity written into the contract, right? Are you talking about morning and afternoon drive?" Lee simply questioned.

"It doesn't matter about the time," Bonner affected a gracious smile. "If he has established credit with us, he can get anything he wants. Remember he's paying a good price for the privilege. In the many years I've been around, I've yet to find an advertiser willing to pay the cost."

"Suppose I was interested. Would my credit be sufficient? If so, it would seem that kind of contract would get a nice package of promote spots, right?" Lee pressed as if he didn't already know the answer.

"Certainly, my friend," Bonner chuckled. "Your credit's good and you name the promote spots, within reason, and I'll write you up personally and hand carry the contract over to The Buhl."

"Very well then," Lee fixed on Bonner's eyes. "I want exclusivity between eight and nine in the mornings and between three and six in the afternoons."

It took a moment for Lee's requests to register with Bonner. When it finally dawned on him, he was struck with his second jolt.

"You mean... I see... I mean you're really serious, aren't you, Mr. Lee?" Bonner said, straightening in his seat, his eyes twitching with excitement. Lee's non-response no longer seemed important. Bonner snatched up the pen and began figuring.

"That's sixteen spots daily, eighty per week," Lee announced. Then he added, "That should get me thirty or more promote spots, right, sir?"

Bonner was befuddled. Still, he nodded hesitantly, not in agreement, but more like he was shaking the confusion clogging his head.

Sensing Bonner's disarray, Lee struck. "I have another request to make. I'm running ads with a couple of other stations under my house agency. I'd like to do the same here—any problems?"

"No, no. Anything you want, my friend. Let me take a few minutes now to get it all down in writing."

"Don't bother, sir. I have the contract here," I said.

That was Bonner's third jolt. He looked up at me as if wondering what's going on, or if he'd heard right.

I handed the contract to him and watched him stir in his seat, as he looked it up and down. Seeing Bonner in this position with so little power, I couldn't help smiling to myself. I'd never thought the time would come when I'd deliberately stoop to belittle my boss, and it did not set easily with me. Still, I was relieved. I needed Bonner to feel the same disappointment and humiliation I'd felt when he betrayed me, not once, but twice. I'd lost confidence in the man, and there was no way I could've continued to work under his helm without taking some kind of action to let Bonner know that I knew he'd wronged me.

"I don't understand," Bonner mumbled. "Except for the promote spots, everything you asked about is already in this contract." Sheepishly, he turned to me and caught my vacant stare of coolness, realizing finally that no clarification was forthcoming.

"I suppose there's nothing left for me to do but sign it," he said, pausing, still anxious to be more involved.

"You can write the bonus spots into the contract; then we'll be all set," Lee said, concluding the matter.

Bonner was smarting from wounded vanity, but I gave him no sympathy. He would've wanted me to sit with him to dot each i and cross each t before going off to make any deal of consequence. But I'd taken his authority and waited as he placed himself in a corner from which his only escape was through the pen. We'd snowed the Snowman, and we left feeling ten feet tall.

Bonner remained bent at his desk, frozen in antagonistic silence as if he'd been slapped in the face, in front of a stranger too. Slowly, he glanced about the office then walked to the dingy window. From his perch, high up on the thirty-first floor, he looked down on the rugged rooftops, and maybe he envisioned tossing me down there. As he mulled over the meeting, he settled on a point: a promise he had made to Lee.

The lines of communication between The Buhl and The Tower were fuzzy. So Bonner figured that since only he and Karl and Henry spoke with them directly, if I did it would only be a conditional probability. With this in mind, Bonner could re-instate his position by turning the contract event in his favor. And no one would be the wiser. What he had in mind would put him on Mr. Beck's good side. So he slipped the contract into his briefcase, snatched his hat and coat from the hook-stand, and rushed to the elevator. On the street, he flagged a cab and rode the six blocks to The Buhl.

Bonner caught Mr. Beck just as the President was about to leave, or so the office ladies who reported all this to me later told me.

"What's your rush, Jerry? You're breathless. Take a seat before you fall out," Beck said, almost fatherly.

Bonner took the nearest seat, holding his chest. It was awfully late for a visit, and Mr. Beck seemed concerned.

"Is everything all right at The Tower?"

"Yes, Mr. Beck. I just wanted to get a contract here before the office closed. One of the salesmen and I have been working diligently for quite awhile to increase this client's budget. We finally did it and it's pretty big. I promised the client I'd personally carry it over here today. You know how important it is to me to keep my word."

Not knowing what pretty big meant, Beck asked to see the contract. Bonner hedged, saying he didn't want to bother him with this, only that he wanted to get the contract delivered to go through the usual channels. Cagily, Bonner let Beck continue to persuade him, building anticipation, as Bonner feigned honest respect. At last he extracted the contract from his briefcase and handed it to Beck, watching for the mounting exhilaration he knew would be emitted anytime now. Bonner waited. He was getting antsy. The seconds turned into minutes, as Beck read some of the pages twice, saying nothing until –

"Wow! This is excellent, Jerry," he finally exclaimed. "I see how much work it must have taken. Congratulations!" The crow's feet at the corners of Beck's eyes were now deeply lined; his teeth, large and even, displayed a horse-like smile. Beck reached for Bonner's hand, not with the usual perfunctory limp shake, an unconscious gesture between more pressing concerns, but this time with a hardy "Congratulations," that he repeated.

With his eyes lit up, Beck called in Ed Butler, and handed him the contract. Slowly and deliberately, Butler looked it over. Now, I'd told Butler I was working on this, and the possibility of this account expanding. Never was Bonner mentioned. Butler agreed he was very much impressed, but he remained stoic. After all, he was facing Bonner, his archenemy. Whenever Beck was away, Bonner would visit The Buhl and ignore Butler, strutting about the office like a four star general inspecting his troops, asking around about matters that were none of his business. Never once, until Bonner got caught up in rumors about being iced, and the possibility of Beck considering adding a VP to Bonner's title, had he given Butler his prospers. No, an accomplishment was the last thing Butler wanted to hear about this man.

Also, the thirty promote spots caught his attention and made him uneasy, but he dared not disparage them for fear of being drawn more into the conversation. Butler handed the contract back to Beck, and forced a nod, not meeting anyone's eyes. But Beck barely noticed Butler's coldness. This was a great moment, no time to be concerned with petty differences.

"Ed," Beck said gleefully, "Jerry must have overheard our earlier talk. With a few more contracts like this, we won't have a problem meeting what we spoke about, right, Ed? Right? Right?" he repeated, nudging Butler's arm. Bonner, like Beck, waited on Butler's confirmation. But Butler was in a bind, knowing he needed some kind of response to give Beck due respect, if nothing else. That Bonner also knew. And while Bonner realized there was no chance of getting kudos from Butler in Beck's (or anyone's) presence, he wanted to at least have his satisfaction with the little bugger's response. After all, this deal was something that had never been done until now.

Butler forced a smile and finally agreed. What else could he do in the face of all of Beck's prompting? But it was a strain, and he abruptly excused himself, not caring a damn if he looked rude. He couldn't stand Bonner's puffed up presence another second, and he wanted Bonner to know it.

Butler returned to his office, and mulled over a question: Why hadn't I mentioned Bonner? Knowing Bonner's track-record, his devious ways, and the less than complimentary reports on his salesmanship from their national rep in New York, he realized there was no way Bonner could have played a major role in this. Suspicious, he decided to check it out.

My phone rang; it was Butler in his high-pitched voice. "I had to call and congratulate you on Lee's contract. It's a dandy. Tell me, what part did Bonner play in getting it?"

That took me by surprise and I asked what he was talking about.

"Did Bonner make calls with you? Did he suggest your approach? What part did he play, if any?"

My mind was spinning. How did Butler know about the hit so quickly? Did Bonner call? If so, did he say he had helped? All I could muster was, "Other than agreeing to the bonus spots and signing the contract, none."

"That's what I thought. Thank you, and keep up the good work. Mr. Beck will be pleased. Maybe the two of us can have lunch with Mr. Lee soon."

Butler hung up, no doubt pleased with himself. From Butler's office, Beck could be seen still consorting with Bonner over the big hit. Butler might have liked to go over there and call Bonner a liar, and say he'll never get the vice-presidency he'd been bucking for. But Butler had a better alternative. He'd allow Bonner the privilege of sustaining his illusion. But he filed away the information he'd just learned from me to use the day he would go for Bonner's jugular.

CHAPTER SIX

Nutall and Company, a small family-run shop, had finished computing the details of a buy for me. Some time back, I'd submitted proposals to Bob, who was the president's son, though I hadn't heard from them in a while. Finally they were ready, so Bob asked Connie, their receptionist, to call me. It would have been simple enough, except for what happened next.

I was out making a speech – around this time I was sometimes invited to present awards or give addresses at civic luncheons, especially when they concerned Negro businesses. I didn't seek out these showcases. In fact, I kept in mind my mother's words, "If you're doing something good, you don't need to talk about it. People will know your good deeds, and they'll come and tell you and everyone about them." Still, my profile in the community was vital to my success, so I usually accepted.

Meanwhile, at The Tower, Beverly, who ran our switchboard, knew I was scheduled to be out speaking, when Connie called. Bonner was killing time in the lobby near the lit-up switchboard, as Beverly struggled to keep up. "No, he hasn't returned yet," Beverly, sounded curt and tense to the caller. "Yes, I already put your first message in his box… Hey!" she realized the caller had hung up on her. Then she noticed the boss was watching. She apologized; it was the second call for me from Nutall so Beverly put a second message in my box to call them.

Bonner claimed he had no idea where to find me, and admonished Beverly, "Don't say a word about this. It should teach him to check in every now and then."

When I returned, Beverly was out on break. I picked up my messages mostly congratulating me on my speech. It wasn't until later, when Beverly checked in with me as she was closing the switchboard, that she reminded me to call Bob Nutall.

I was bewildered, and fingered through the messages again. "I don't have anything from them. When did they call?"

"While you were out—twice. Are you sure you don't have them?"

"Positive."

Beverly couldn't imagine what happened to the messages, but left my line open. I phoned Bob immediately. No answer. I re-dialed. Nothing. I hung up, disturbed, and left for my crib.

Though Bob and I enjoyed an excellent relationship, he wasn't one to call for trivia. Since he'd tried twice, I knew it was important. Maybe he wanted to close the deal? Regardless, the mystery of the missing messages bugged me throughout the night.

The following day, I raced down the freeway, sprang out of my ride, waved to the parking attendant, and hurried into Nutall and Company.

Connie was surprised. "Was there a problem with the package?"

"What package, sweetheart?" I said at a loss.

"The package your boss picked up yesterday."

"Mr. Bonner?"

"He came over right after I called you the second time. He said he always wanted to meet Bob and his dad, and had been asking you to introduce him. Since he had no idea what time you'd be back, he took a chance and dropped by. It was a little odd the way he kept insisting he wanted to be of help, and he wanted to know everything."

Dreading, I asked, "What did Bob do?"

She shrugged, "Gave him the package, and said to tell you to get back to him. That's it."

"I knew nothing about it," I said, feeling helpless, especially when it turned out Bob and his dad wouldn't even be in the office that day.

I'd always liked Connie's company. Nearly six feet tall, she seemed to relax with me, maybe because I was taller even when she wore heels. Years before, she'd confided that she came from an Italian family and had moved from the Big Apple to the Motor City to get hitched, but broke it off when she found out her fiancé was irresponsible. That's the kind of easy talk we'd always shared, a light flirtation that wasn't meant to be taken to heart. So I didn't mind letting her see I was worried, and took a seat to get my bearings, while Connie brewed coffee. Still processing what happened, I idly watched her put finishing touches on her face. She said, "I'm pissed, not with you, but the rudeness of your damn operator."

"Beverly, rude? That's not like her."

"She was very short with me, and the only reason I could think of was that I called twice. But so what?"

"She's not that type. I'll speak to her…"

"No, please don't. If you say she's not that type, that's good enough for me."

"You're a sweetheart," I said, kissing her cheeks.

"There you go, messing up my make up. Stop it. Stop it," she giggled.

She placed a cup of coffee before me, but I couldn't stop thinking about the package and what it might contain. I had to get out of there.

I approached The Tower, uneasily anticipating what I might expect from Bonner. But Beverly caught me first, apologizing, "The switchboard was jammed and Mr. Bonner was distracting me. I would never be rude intentionally to anyone's client. Well, maybe Karl's," she smiled devilishly, "but never to anybody calling for you."

I glanced in my mailbox and tried to sound casual, "Did Bonner mention anything to you, like he wanted to see me or he had something for me?"

"Unh-unh, nothing."

All possible defenses for Bonner's actions were now exhausted, leaving me dumbfounded. But then, why should I be surprised? This was Bonner's nature I'd grown to know and dislike over the years. He'd never asked to meet Bob and his dad. On top of that, Bonner knew perfectly well where I was yesterday and when I'd be back.

A laundry list of questions popped in my head: Why hadn't Bonner told me about the messages? What happened to them? Why hadn't he left a message that he'd gone to Nutall? Had he wanted to make me appear unreliable? If so, Bonner couldn't make that stick with any of my clients; I had long-standing credibility with them, whereas Bonner was just an unknown with a questionable title. Above all, what I really couldn't understand was why Bonner had to equivocate about so many insignificant things. The more I thought about the ridiculous circumstances, the angrier I became. And I was not about to sit on my hands until Bonner got around to me.

At my desk, I picked up the phone then set it back in place. This was a hard call. It must be done suddenly, face to face. No way was I about to be passive this time – I'd paid my dues and had seen enough. I'd surprise Bonner and force the issue so he wouldn't be able to fudge or beat around the bush. I flipped through my folder of weekly projects and pulled the one I wanted. It was time to lock horns.

I approached Bonner's office from his lobby door so no one would be aware of this impending confrontation. Anxiety mounting, I knocked, harder than usual. The door swung open. Bonner looked surprised but managed a smile.

"I'm glad it's you," he said, taking the initiative as if that might diffuse my anger. "Have a seat. I was about to give you a call when you knocked. I got some good news for you, my boy. I bet you can't guess what."

"Easy – a package you got yesterday from Nutall and Company," I replied dryly, still standing.

"How did you know?" he asked with a look of innocence.

"It's up to me to know what goes on in my business. Don't you suppose I keep in touch with my people so if Karl or anyone else tries to put crap in the game I'll be on top of it?"

"Just what do you mean by that?"

Bonner had bitten my bait, and I was determined to roll out all the misdeeds and games I'd endured. I asked Bonner if he wanted to be taken to church, and then I let go with the way Bonner had stabbed me in the back two times before in political disputes with Karl, and those had drained whatever respect I'd held for him.

"The first time," I reminded him, "though I did all the preliminary work and brought in the contract with proof, you ruled against me, saying Karl's phone confirmation was as good as a signed contract. That, I now know, was bull.

"The problem the second time was when the call came to pick up a contract, and I was out of the office addressing a business meeting, Karl took my message and turned in the order under his name. Again, my daily reports verified my work. Plus, everyone here knew I'd been working on the account. When Karl and I came to you, I explained the circumstances, and even reminded you of your last ruling. Well, you conveniently had a lapse of memory and denied knowing anything about it. You ruled against me once more. At first I was shocked, but then anger hit me. Not only did you take the wind out of my sail, you reopened an old wound and poured salt into it."

I paused, but by no means was I about to end. My furor was rising. I explained I didn't want to do anything rash, and only through raw discipline was I able to reach deep within myself to hold back my rage. I went on that even with our previous differences and Bonner's proclivity for memory lapses to which he never confessed, I held out that Bonner might have regard for his own rules of basic fair play. But I didn't believe that any more.

Emotions were running on a jagged edge. Bonner's face was crimson with indignation. What's gotten into this boy, he seemed to think. Did I forget to whom I was speaking? Lord knows, if Bonner could get away with it, he would have fired me on the spot for insolence.

"I don't have to listen to this affront to my dignity," Bonner snapped. "I make my judgments as I see them. That's why I'm in this seat. Besides, you should've told me your gripe then. There's nothing I can do about it now.

"It may surprise you that when I opened my door and saw you I thought we'd have a pleasant meeting. I'm sorry you feel the way you do. I try to be useful and do the best I can. That's why I went out of my way to Nutall – to do you a favor. I wasn't trying to use you, but if you think I was, I'm sorry."

Of course, I understood that being used was a daily occurrence in the world of business—'you scratch my back, I'll scratch yours'—and I had no problem with that. But to be misused as though I didn't have any semblance of gray matter was untenable.

I said, "What you don't seem to understand is that I'm no longer window dressing to show my face on cue, nor am I a patsy to assist others to sell. I'm a rational, sensitive man, and there's no excuse for you or anyone to take me for granted.

"I can appreciate you looking out for me by picking up the business, even though this copy of my weekly projection I have here clearly shows where I'd be and the time I'd be back. What I don't appreciate is that you'd deliberately confiscate my messages and go about business in a sneaky, unconscionable way."

I paused for effect and then cited, "'O, what a tangled web we weave when first we practice to deceive.' I'm sure you've heard that verse by Sir Walter Scott, right?" I didn't wait for a reply to bring home the point, "Were you planning to use this package the same way you used Lee's contract?"

Shocked, Bonner sputtered, "I don't understand how that quote relates to me. What messages are you referring to? And what does this have to do with Lee's contract?"

"The messages you saw," I lashed back. "You admitted to Connie they prompted you to go over there. As for Lee's contract, I heard that you took it over to The Buhl and claimed you played an important role in getting it. You know what that quote is about."

Still standing, I was full of defiance, threatening, as my icy stare cut through Bonner's composure. He'd always thought of me as mannerly and demure. For the first time he faced me as a man asserting his position, on the offensive, far from the passive reaction Bonner expected. And now he was cornered because everything I said was true. If he didn't acquiesce, I certainly wasn't going to bend. And by no means did he want me to take my concern to Mr. Beck and expose a side of him he needed to remain hidden.

"You're right. I did see the messages. In fact, I thought I'd put them back in your box. But as for Lee's contract, I don't understand. It was handled in the usual fashion. But be that as it may, if my feeble old age made me negligent, please forgive me," he implored. "It was an honest mistake."

I had no reason to forgive him, and not for one second did I buy his attempt to explain away his surreptitious behavior. Bonner had exposed himself for what he really was – an unscrupulous hypocrite, a pretentious, shoddy little man without honor. I peered deeply into his eyes, searching to find his inner soul. Only when I saw capitulation across his face was I satisfied. I'd delivered my *coup de grace*. No need to prolong this clash.

"Where's the package?" I asked, still standing.

"Right here on my desk. I kept it handy so I wouldn't misplace it before giving it to you. Sit down, and get comfortable. When you open it, I bet you'll be as surprised as I was."

"Thanks, but I prefer standing at this point."

I unfolded the instructions. They read, "Please combine a schedule of 60 second spots totaling two thousand dollars per week for Premiere Furniture Company and Prime Furniture. Schedule equal number of spots for both and rotate enclosed copy accordingly. Start date: ASAP. End date: TF. Have confirmation in my office by my return."

Slowly, I folded back the instructions and replied in a matter-of-fact tone, "It's a little less than I'd expected. But, all in all, it's a decent hit."

"You're not saying you presented a proposal bigger than this, are you?"

"Why not," I lied, attempting to quell Bonner's enthusiasm. I didn't want him to feel any redemption or to let him off the hook. But in truth the contract's timing couldn't have been more providential, and the package couldn't have been more substantial.

As I turned away, I never let up on my intense resolution, and privately determined that small-minded men like Bonner would pale in the years to come. I'd found peace with myself, and I left quietly with an unexpected sense of gratitude, relieved of the burdensome passions I had shouldered much too long.

Back at my desk, I sat in thought for a moment and then dialed Butler. I was confident I'd forged the kind of relationship I wanted with Butler, but the time had come to test it and see whose side he would take.

"Did Bonner claim some part of a contract I'd gotten yesterday?" I asked Butler directly. I told him how I'd confronted Bonner and added, "He's probably trying, right now, to figure out some way to fire me."

"Don't give that another thought," Butler said. "You did the right thing. If anyone goes, it'll be him not you. I can promise you that. Keep in touch."

I was near euphoria. With the right answer from Butler and the contracts in hand, I couldn't stay still. Quickly, I made out the orders and left The Tower. I needed some space to walk about, to sizzle some of the irrepressible excitement bubbling through my veins.

Pumped up and filled with joy, I walked through Grand Circus Park, touching my hat brim to the ladies and nodding to the men, imagining the three c-notes I would earn each week in commissions from the contracts. Along with the business I'd already established, that came to four times the chump-change the cats on the block were bragging about handling. My commercial load would now exhaust much of the Negro-programmed shows. I was top dog, high man on the totem pole, and I had even better aims in mind as soon as the time would be right.

CHAPTER SEVEN

Stokely Carmichael's call for "Black Power" created a vast whirlwind that swept rapidly over the country. The young leader of SNCC (Student Non-violent Coordinating Committee) had used that phrase in his speech at the Meredith March through Mississippi. But in 1966 the white press made no attempt to understand, and reacted instead with alarm, unleashing a media blitz that twisted Stokely's words.

If the general media misconstrued Black Power to mean anti-white actions including violence, the Negro press and its communities knew the true intention. Black Power meant equal opportunities for jobs, health, and education, and Negro control of their own communities. But it became clear that the powers were not willing to consider any of that, only to wait. "Wait"—that word which Dr. King said, "rings in the ear of every Negro with a piercing familiarity that has almost always meant 'never.'"

While the general media continued to snap at the question of Black Power, I felt compelled to spend more time in this new environment, renewing my sense of my market. First, I took interest in local elected offices, and found they consisted of one City Councilman, two judges, a couple of State Senators, eight State Representatives, and two U.S. Congressmen.

Though the elected representatives were limited, I discovered that the teachings of Malcolm X and the growing sense of Black Power had set in motion a revolution in the minds of many in my market. People were becoming more comprehensive in thinking, more selective about whom they'd patronize, and more vocal if their civil liberties or fair employment were denied. They were politicizing themselves, learning the system of government, even running for a number of offices under either the controversial all-Negro "Freedom Now Party" that advocated an all-Negro slate, or the Democratic Party's liberal reform slate pushed by some of the old guard.

I'd helped out in a few campaigns, but I wasn't a man of any one party. As an extension of my work, I was able to mingle comfortably among all the politicians, the movers and shakers and the political hacks, at venues supporting one special concern or another, and at various socials. I enjoyed my role as a maverick, able to express my opinions openly without being beholden to anyone.

By this time, three stations including The Tower now vied for my market. WTAG came with nothing unique in format and aroused little competitive concern. However, WDEE, the sister station of WDDD, received a license to operate and was filling its airwaves with the original classic jazz of such famed greats as Dizzy, Press, Bird, Coltrane, Miles, Dexter, Monk, Moody and the like. So WDEE was now claiming a segment of the total market that no station had catered to before.

Beyond that, Negro-owned WDDD had made some important improvements and was no longer a sun-up to sundown station. Now licensed to air around-the-clock, it was positioned to take full advantage of any listeners The Tower had gained before our Polish-speaking program commenced at 6:00 p.m. Along with its new "soul radio" station-break jingles that directly related to the spirit of my market, and its hip, rhythmic-talkin' jocks, WDDD bristled with Motown hits. It aired the purest of soul into the wee hours, captivating and satiating my market in the areas it covered.

Most impressive, a particular woman at WDDD who had come right up from Memphis, Tennessee, calling herself "Her Majesty" was somp'un else. "To be touched by Her Majesty," she would say on the air, "will put you into somp'un that you can't shake loose, I betcha."

She brought an earthiness bereft of any hint of refinement; in her voice the audience felt the profoundness of painful memories of a marriage gone sour that left her to rear three young daughters alone. Her nemeses were the colored men. Spiced with down-home humor and dripping with sarcasm, she hit the air a few years back and came down hard on the men. With one fell swoop, from the blue-collar workers to the jack-legged preachers, sparing none in between, she lambasted the brothers the way the "signifying monkey" ridiculed the lion in the traditional story we all knew.

She was criticized, misunderstood and maligned in whispers, but that didn't faze her veneer. She remained impervious and undaunted, though an attentive ear could detect that deep down inside, hidden away from inquisitive eyes, resentment stewed. Nonetheless, she just kept keeping on as though obsessed, battering the men-folk and thumbing her nose at the highbrows, and, in time, gaining allies who related to what she'd been through and had an affinity for her off-the-wall, brazen ways.

I viewed her in two lights. As one of her male listeners, I, too, had felt stings of embarrassment that her broad portrayals served only to perpetuate the downgraded stereotypes that some perplexed Negro women maintained about Negro men. In those crushing moments, I thought it was imperative to qualify her remarks; I wanted to admonish her, to make her acknowledge that not all men were so un-ready. I also believed my market was far more sophisticated than what she'd been used to in the South.

Yet, in another light, as a salesman, I defended her, brushing off her broad indictments of brothers as merely impulsive, extemporaneous blunders. I heard her exercising extraordinary on-air salesmanship, sharing her personal frustrations and joys to gain ears, relaxing listeners to the point they were drawn up in her mystique. But I felt ambiguous, even about this reaction. To tell the gospel truth, when riled up by a call-in, she became extremely vindictive to the point that I had to hurry over to turn down the volume, for the kilocycles shook in her thunder. At those times, the term "country" wouldn't be adequate to describe her wrath. Scandalous would be more fitting.

Even so, with all her impetuous temperament, I dug her genuinely from day one. She came across like family – such as a mother mindful of thought-provoking common sense, or a set-minded argumentative sister. Sometimes she seemed like a benevolent sweetheart cooing words of endearment, and at other times a frisky street-broad whose lips dripped with meaningless jive that led me to a vivid fantasy of one day hustling her time.

I made Bonner aware of Her Majesty, stressing the importance of having her in our camp. But Bonner shrugged it off as not worth of any exploration. "After all," Bonner said, "women are being phased out of the media not in."

I kept pressing, explaining the competitive changes occurring in the Negro market, and cautioned him about their significance. At least take the jack-legged preachers off the air, I advised. Better yet, switch the foreign language programs of The Tower to our sister station to counteract WDDD's recent move to twenty-four hour programming. But Bonner ignored these suggestions also.

Meanwhile, the spot-sells in the Negro programs were up and consistent because of my deals. Karl's jack-legged preachers – frowned on by most of my market, and considered insulting – were standing in line to gobble up any segment of time that might become available. Bonner's head was in the clouds, having come off his best year ever, and greed took precedence over foresight. Bonner permitted eleven to thirteen commercial spots to be logged on the half-hour in the Negro-programmed segments, disregarding FCC regulations that called for nine at most. This overload offended and turned off many in The Tower's audience who listened to be entertained and informed, not bombarded with commercial hype. But because of Bonner's distance from the newly enlightened more active Negro market, he lacked the vision that was needed to deal with the effects all the changes would soon have on the profitability of The Tower.

Communication between us became abysmal. Feeling contempt for Bonner's authority, I bugged him with a mind-game I'd once played as a kid, handling him with a cautious politeness, which I reserved for those strangers whose onerous reputation had preceded them. I offered meaningless remarks and exchanged tentative nods, but never did I pretend a smile.

I had to attend the sales meetings, where at one time I'd taken particular pride in contributing substance. But now I merely appeared and responded "no comment" when asked for my thoughts. I couldn't stand being in Bonner's presence and figured the meetings would deteriorate in the absence of my constructive input, and I was right on the money. Soon the meetings came to be without purpose, without direction, and ridiculously boring to everyone.

Bonner sensed what I was up to, and it must have become apparent that he'd been outwitted at every turn in his attempts to manipulate me. He had misjudged my tenacity, though that quality of mine had inadvertently helped Bonner secure his very own position. He needed to mend fences and reconcile with me. But I wouldn't have it; I'd made a silent resolve never to consult with him again.

Desperate to regain my cooperation, Bonner came up with what he thought was a bright idea to get the unbearable meetings back on track. Each salesman was assigned a date on which to open the meetings with some thought provoking message which the others could discuss and build upon. I was first in line, and readily recognized Bonner's game. I had no choice but to participate, but how could I work in clear conscience with a man I so deeply mistrusted?

I returned to my crib to think over my relationships with my fellow workers. My apartment looked like an extension of my office – folders of information, news clippings, notes to myself for things to do, proposals, calculations on packages, contact phone numbers all lay in piles of papers on the floors, tables and chairs. I came here only to think, sleep, bathe, change clothes and go out again; it wasn't a show place. Besides my family photos – especially my mother and sisters—and a few publicity shots of me giving speeches, and my wardrobe (I always did appreciate quality clothes), not much here looked personal. Still, it was my refuge.

I felt secure that under the circumstances my relationships within the sales department were as good as could be expected. Karl was what he was, a bore, a parasite, certainly not a salesman, and Bonner had plenty of evidence of that by now. I thought about the others, and concluded they weren't real problems, either. The difficulty lay with Bonner who cast aspersions on everyone and created an atmosphere of suspicion and deceit with his snide innuendoes as he oversaw sales. Why all the games? What real purpose could they serve? I thought sales needed to take a good look at it and undergo some type of behavior modification. It needed its character shaken up, and I had the urge to do it, to hit squarely at Bonner and Karl. And I wanted to accomplish that with dignity, grace and style.

Two weeks later, the salesmen gathered back in Bonner's office and waited in silence as he finished his call. Bonner laid the receiver on its cradle and smoothed over his desk pad, his customary habit, before looking up to me.

"I, no less than the others, have been eagerly awaiting this day," Bonner said solemnly. "I'm confident that after all your weeks of silence you have something to offer that will have a lasting affect on all of us for some time to come."

I'd anticipated that sort of solemnity and thought Bonner's respect should've been shown long before in his actions. But it didn't matter any more. Today I was going to tell them exactly where I was coming from.

I stood and began, "You all know my purpose today. But what you don't know is that in coming up with my thoughts for this day I had to reach way back to the genesis, when I was a little boy being raised by my mother. I wondered how I could best capture the essence of my early legacy to explain who I am and what I feel today. After some time, it came to me to put it in verse. I've named this 'A Molder of Character.'" With calm decisiveness, I recited by memory:

"I'm a proud man, a proud man who's proud of his heritage, a proud man who's proud of his color. Not the man who's proud of his dress but not of his honor, nor the man who's proud of his wit but not of his word, but a proud man. I won't take from you if you take from me, but I'll watch you like a hawk. I don't mingle with frivolous characters or listen to their talk. But I'll stand tall, stare them dead in the eyes, and before long, I'll take a walk. 'Cause I'm a proud man, proud in all respects of the word. And if all men were proud like this, man could not wrong. I'm a proud man."

At suitable intervals, I gazed at Bonner and at Karl. Their reactions were more gratifying than I'd dared to anticipate, more than enough to convince me that my message had gotten through. Before I started my introduction, Bonner was tilted back in his high cushioned chair, the back of his head cupped in his hands. He had a smug gloat on his face that insinuated 'I gotchu where I wanchu, baby.' By the time I ended, he was bent at his desk frozen in nullified silence.

Karl, on the other hand, was now sitting stiffly, vexation clouding his ruddy face. The pen with which he'd been doodling had slipped from his fingers and was rolling aimlessly at his foot.

Henry was the only one not still as a mannequin. Awe-struck, he shook my hand in agreement and made an effort to repeat some lines to get a dialogue going. But it was all in vain. Pretending the call he'd gotten earlier demanded his immediate attention, Bonner abruptly ended the meeting.

Despite the crude reception I'd gotten, I felt I'd depicted myself as I'd wanted while uncloaking the false principles of Bonner and Karl, and made it clear I wasn't someone they could mess over, but a man who could retaliate with mental abilities more deeply polished than they possessed. Moreover, they saw I was a man who could undress them without flinching and leave them cowering in their unmasked nakedness.

In the July/August ratings sweep, Pulse's book (the principle rating service to which The Tower subscribed) showed that WDDD's audience share was greater than The Tower's, even though The Tower's non-directional signal made its total area coverage much larger. The book burst Bonner's bubble and jolted the other salesmen. With their inadequate knowledge of the Negro market, they didn't want to accept Pulse's findings, for to do so would eliminate their only sales tool, but they had no choice.

Bonner hit the panic button as The Tower struggled with its shortcomings. The programming became erratic as jocks from afar came and went by the month, sometimes by the week, as The Tower desperately attempted to find the right combination of personalities to regain its lost audience and counter its precipitous drop in sales.

For the first time, in the wake of The Tower's fiasco, Mr. Beck called a meeting with members of his board and the sales department at its headquarters. I knew little about Beck except what I got from second-hand talk, and because the talk had come mainly from Bonner and Karl I didn't give it much credence. Now I was anticipating taking a good look at the man, and at the same time seeing Bonner's smallness under the weight of his incompetence.

Entering The Buhl office, I noticed the antique gun collection inside a large showcase just to the right of the door. It afforded me a conversation piece to loosen up the stiffness before the meeting started. The large offices were as I'd pictured—conservative, decorated in contemporary taste, a far cry from the World War II-remnant furnishings that were jammed into the small offices at The Tower.

No sooner had the meeting commenced, I was stunned by a reference I never would have expected in such a setting. Beck revealed his extreme naiveté of the market, which engendered the lion's share of income for his biggest moneymaker by using the word "nigras." Actually, I doubted he said it in disrespect because it came with no hesitation, his face hinting neither guilt nor embarrassment. It was merely his natural way of speaking, which demonstrated clearly how far removed his world was from mine.

I said nothing. I had come with the intent of saying nothing, only to assiduously observe, be cool, keep an open mind, and get a fix on this man to satisfy my long-standing curiosity. But in spite of my intentions, each time Beck said "nigras" my insides cringed until I thought to myself, "What kinda shit is this! No wonder Bonner's insufficiencies go ungoverned; there's absolutely no one in authority who knows enough to check the fool out."

Beck stood adamantly against the change to an all-Negro format because it would require switching his floundering foreign-language programs to his FM station. "The move," he said, "would amount to a loss of two hundred thousand dollars in revenue that FM currently books."

I was surprised the subject even came up. It showed that Bonner or someone must have thought enough of my earlier suggestion to pass it on to Beck. Anyway, I thought that if Beck had been cognizant of the Negro market, he would've realized that the FM loss was a mere pittance compared to the ten-fold increase in monies The Tower would turn with a consistent round-the-clock format geared to the Negro audience.

Bonner made no attempt to respond to Beck's statement. In fact, he appeared to have no scrimmages in mind, though some sort of plan had been rumored. Rather, he just seemed glad to have the attention focus on something other than himself, a knack he was very good at.

As expected, the two bespectacled board members, Edward Butler and Lawrence Roberts, were in the "Amen corner." Aside from the two hundred grand Beck cited, what did they know? After every other sentence, Beck called on the board members for an affirmation and got it every time.

I was struck by the irony. Never, since leaving the service, had I heard such litanies of "yes sirs." The absurdity of the meeting was mind-boggling and the whole pathetic scene would have been a laugh if my vision of my future had not begun to cloud.

Growing up, I'd heard stories about what went on in the dark times of Mother Dear's youth, when hooded faces intimidated the Southern countryside. It was crystal clear who owned the plantation now and that these men were mere vessels through which Beck's orders were played out. It would be pure folly to waste any more time considering matters in which I'd have no meaningful voice.

After that reality check, I felt I was cleared of any concern for The Tower, as I reeled with disgust. I dismissed the meeting from my mind and allowed my thoughts to wander to the many job offers I'd gotten from in and out of town even from people I didn't know who had heard of my professionalism. Several of the offers had just been "feelers," but my strong rapport with some members of the agencies suggested I would be able to land somewhere quite well. Yet I had too much time invested in The Tower to simply walk away.

All the same, I needed a legitimate reason to stay put and use this place to my advantage. I mused over several possibilities. Then I got a wake up call: I needed to challenge the system. And in order to do that, I needed a confederate – someone who was bold and fearless. I needed someone I could trust to bear some of my burden.

CHAPTER EIGHT

Several days later on the Westside of the city, the folks in the Chitchat Lounge were in an exuberant mood. In the thick of it was Her Majesty, getting ready to MC her Tuesday night show. Full-figured, tall and light complexioned, to the slick city cats, she was too hot to trot, and to the down-home country brothers, she was a "stone cold yellow hammer!"

She strutted her stuff to and fro across the stage, her big yellow yams showing beneath her short skirt. Turning to the house, she questioned, "Who wants to be touched by Her Majesty?" Up went several hands, and two brothers dashed to the stage.

She stopped at center stage. Holding the microphone in one hand, she placed her other on her hip, and as her hips began to wiggle, she tossed come-on glances at the two then cracked a teasing smile.

"Are you two sure you can handle Her Majesty's touch?" she taunted. "You look kinda poorly. And as most folks here know, it'll put you into somp'un that you can't shake loose, I betcha."

The two brothers insisted, giggling and bowing in jest with outstretched hands. She touched them, one by one. They seemed to become electrified and began to hop about like jackrabbits. The house roared. Her Majesty smiled. It was now show time!

I was at the bar joining in on the merriment while jawing with the bartender and some of the regulars. After a while, I moved to a table just left of the stage to collect my thoughts and pursue my purpose for being there. Rumors on the industry's grapevine hinted of a rift between WDDD and Her Majesty. She wanted more freedom of expression and to expand her show; however, she wanted to remain in the city. If the rumors and her desires were accurate, this could be my opportunity to act on something I wanted and, at the same time, possibly gain an ally.

I had phoned Her Majesty and arranged to talk with her tonight between sets. I'd also gotten permission from the proprietor (who was one of my clients) to use her office to meet. So when the set ended, I stepped over to the office door and waited.

The jukebox was blaring as Her Majesty left the stage, and several couples were now gettin' down on the dance floor. I watched her as she threaded through the crowd, chatting briefly or shrugging away from hands that reached out at her. When she finally got to me, she sighed deeply, entered the office, and sat on the couch. Immediately, she pulled off her high heel kicks and began massaging her feet.

She asked me to excuse her informality but those damn shoes were killing her poor dogs. Frowning, she asked, "Why meet at this place on this of all days? We could've had lunch or met someplace where I wouldn't be heckled by so many drunks talking about I'm not ready for the revolution. What revolution? Have you heard anything so ridiculous? I get so damn tired of drunks hanging all over me, talkin' their shit. They seem to think that it's their privilege. I don't have time for that kind of crap. One day, I hope to put these damn shows behind me."

I apologized—had I known she felt that way I would've suggested some other place. At the time, I wasn't sure she would remember me and come elsewhere, and I thought meeting here would be more convenient for her.

She sighed heavily, "Hey child, it's all right. You'll have to excuse my attitude but that's the way I feel. Now tell me, honey child, what's up?"

"I heard you're looking for greener pastures."

She said I'd heard right. She'd been screaming to get out of WDDD. She was tired of the hassles, tired of fighting with ownership and that no account Donald Lacey.

"What's wrong with him? He seems to be all right."

"Forget him, man." After a moment she added stiffly, "That's a long story. Now what about greener pastures? You got something up?"

"Could be if you care to listen."

"I'm here ain't I? Now don't take all day, child. You know I got another show to do, so get crackin' and get to the point."

I told her if she really wanted to increase her audience and do her *thang* in town, she should be thinking about The Tower. I explained The Tower's predicament, then said, "Excuse my language, lady, but they don't know their asses from a hole in the ground. They're in deep shit and they don't know why, or how to get out of it."

"I suppose you know," she said with a touch of sarcasm.

"I sure do, lady. Now, if you care to listen and keep your sarcasm to yourself, I'll continue."

"Go on, man," she grumbled impatiently.

I told her of the greed, the bad management and the overloading of commercial spots. Then I told her that Bonner fired Soul Man, a jock who'd delighted his audience instantly and been instrumental in attracting thousands of new listeners to The Tower.

"Excuse me, but I heard that Soul Man lost interest," she said.

I agreed that he'd lost some of his old spark, but I chalked that up to the quibbles over the promised raise he never received and the lack of respect management had shown him. The overriding reason Bonner let him go was Bonner's ego. "Understand," I said, "Bonner's the boss, the captain of the ship, and he doesn't want anyone to doubt that."

"I'm hearing there's no love lost between you and this Bonner person, right?"

I confided in her about how he wouldn't allow his judgments to be questioned even if they were wrong. "Not having been raised to accept wrong, my straightforward convictions against wrong have become even stronger. And arrogance is not my style…"

"Oh really?" she interrupted, her eyebrows raised, her nose sloping in air at a forty-five degree angle.

I told her I didn't need to massage my own ego. It's just that I'd grown into a certain assuredness that made it impossible for me to salute smartly and turn an about face on my heels at Bonner's nonsensical commands, though Bonner considered this refusal to be reprehensible conduct. Because of my attitude, and my candid opinions on the industry, which were contrary to Bonner's, he would have iced me as well as Soul Man. But he couldn't fire me because I was the chief go-getter of new business. Bonner couldn't risk another drop in sales.

She asked what affect the Pulse ratings had on me. I told her none whatsoever. I sold from facts and the heart, not from the book. I wasn't much of a believer in rating systems anyway, not in that one or Hooper's or Nielsen's or any other because none of them were conceived with our market in mind. But I was amongst the market every day, and had my finger on its heartbeat, so I could sense the downfall coming all along.

"What's more," I emphasized, "I know the nuances of my market. I realize it includes some prudish folks who wear their affluence on their sleeves and would never own up to their preference for Negro radio."

"Why?" she chimed in.

"Too scared their air of sophistication would be tarnished in the eyes of the pollster if they admitted listening."

"Well, I'll be damned! I've been saying the same thing all along – only I put it in much stronger terms. I wouldn't call them sophisticated. I'd call them snooty fools who can't wipe their funky asses without instructions!"

"You don't bite your tongue at all," I laughed.

"Why should I? We're both adults, right?"

I agreed and closed in on my pitch: It would be a snap – all she had to do was go! She could get anything she wanted out of WTOP. I'd already spoken to Ed Butler, the controller, who had the ear of ownership. And I'd personally look forward to selling her, if she were interested. I pulled a card from my breast pocket and handed it to her. I then told her I'd taken the liberty to tell Butler that she would call.

"Well, man," she replied, "you seem to be straight up. You came prepared. That's the only reason I'm still sitting here. Plus, I like your style, honey child. Yes, I'm interested."

I'd lied. I hadn't talked to Butler. So the next day I got on the horn with him. We met at our usual place, the coffee shop. I tried every way I could to persuade him on Her Majesty, pointing out her qualities and insisting that Butler do himself a favor and hear her out when she calls. But Butler said he'd already discussed her with Bonner, and he agreed with Bonner that women are being faded out of the business.

"You're right as far as the general radio and TV," I argued. "But Negro women are the backbone in Negro society, and they're regarded as indispensable. Besides, our competitors are utilizing women's talents with a great deal of success. With the state that The Tower's sales are in, she's a damn good find."

"Do you really think she's that good?"

"Sir, would I be sitting here with you if I didn't?"

"If I do what you're asking, I'll be depending on your words alone."

I convinced him he wouldn't have any regrets.

Not long afterward, Her Majesty was sitting snug and straight against the back of a chair facing Bonner at his desk. She crossed her big yellow yams and tussled with her short skirt to cover as much of her thighs as the skirt would give.

Bonner twisted and turned in his seat, having never been in a position to judge such an attractive, imposing woman, especially a colored one. She was looking good and smelling good as his eyes glanced here and there, trying to avoid staring. He seemed more like a fumbling teenaged boy meeting his girlfriend's parents for the first time.

Her Majesty was aware of Bonner's predicament. I'd schooled her well. To play out her hand, this was exactly the impression she intended to make as she exuded composure, much different from the carefree, down to earth facade that came across during her weekly shows. Her life of twists and turns was serious business, necessitating ongoing changes of style. Having internalized, some years back, that this world belonged to white men, she had honed a natural way of dealing with them. Whether the men were weak, strong or in between, her attributes and her old Southern airs (which she affected by design) were chosen to tap most men's desires. Those qualities carried her through the South to here, and at no time had she used the couch to gain her purpose.

"You have a nice tidy office, Mr. Bonner," she said softly, uncrossing her legs, taking the initiative to break through the silence.

"Oh, thank you. It's almost a little too small," he said in an apologetic tone, his eyes cast down to his hand smoothing over his desk pad. "But I like it like this. I don't need much. Just give me enough room to take care of my affairs and I'm happy," he fumbled on with a tentative smile.

She inquired about the gentleman in the picture on the wall. The turn Bonner made to face it wasn't necessary; he knew who was pictured there. But he saw it as a good chance to recover from the tension that was straining him.

"Oh," he said, "That's the owner, Mr. Beck."

"What's his thinking about women in radio?"

"It doesn't matter. I do the hiring," he answered cavalierly, turning back to her.

"Oh, I see. Then tell me your thoughts," she prodded, remembering what I'd said.

"Contrary to many in the business, I believe there's a place for them. I've said that a number of times at gatherings where I was asked to speak," he lied ever so smoothly, determined to put his best face on.

"Have you had a chance to check out my show?" she asked, well aware that was unlikely because few whites in management of Negro radio had felt the need to actually listen to their product.

"No, but, in a manner of speaking, yes. That is, since I've heard so many wonderful things about you and your show, I feel as if I have. That's why when Mr. Butler and I had a talk about you recently I agreed to have you come in."

"Then tell me, what would you be looking for from me if I were to come?"

He smiled graciously but didn't know enough about the market to have any specific ideas, so he responded in generalities: He'd expect her to have a fine reputation in the community, to be entertaining enough to build and hold an audience, and to be respectful, accountable, responsible and cooperative. "But most important," he said as he leaned forward, his voice feigning humility, "to be a good friend. I need someone I can confide in and feel that my words won't be betrayed," he said ruefully. It was the same tired, rehearsed words he'd spoken to me when we had our first lone meeting.

She looked at him long and hard from across the desk and he looked back at her. "Well, Mr. Bonner," she said, crossing her yellow yams slowly, drawing his eyes to them, "you're talking to the right person, if we can get together. You see, sir, you got all of that in me and much more."

Her Majesty, a masterful excavator of human impotencies, could seize a man and pummel him into submission. This poor widow woman from the South had long ago envisioned herself traversing the river Nile with a queenly crown upon her head. Like Caesar, she came, saw and conquered Bonner, whose perplexity was in dire need of her honey-tongued consultation. She'd charmed him out of his pants then twisted his bareness around her pinkie, inducing from him all that she had wanted for her services.

With her colorful "Tasting Time" segment, an upbeat salute to those who worked by the sweat of their brows, and her spiritual-styled "Inspirational Time," a ten-minute segment imparting words of encouragement to the lonely and downtrodden, her show took on the likeness of a daily soap opera. She brought a new dimension to The Tower's programming, and with it, a brand new audience into The Tower's fold.

Having waited such a long time for the privilege to sell her, I had to get even closer without crowding her. I needed to know what drove her in order to frame the proper sketch to sell her as a valuable commodity—and more important, to see if I could trust her to be my ally.

When time permitted, I shed my three-piece suit and tie, as though cleansing my soul of all its material indulgences. I wriggled into my tight denim jeans, and snatched up my jacket on the run. I joined Her Majesty and her workers and went to some of her fans that were living just above the streets, touching them with uplifting words. It was somewhere in those benign faces filled with gratitude that the thirst that drove me to her was quenched. I saw her not as the "freewheeling bitch," as some had come to judge her, but rather a fertile thinker, well focused.

Her strong vision of what it really meant to have stature and her determination to be revered by powerful people were part of what drove her. For that reason, I wasn't too sure she was truly as committed as she claimed to the "little folks," who were mostly humble, gullible and easy to manipulate. I even wondered whether her main objective in seeking them out and embracing them as her own was to build a base from which to realize her regal dreams.

I now considered her a friend – a guarded, business friend. Still, the thoughts of her real intent continued to be entwined in questions I posed to myself. If she's using them—so what! What good is Her Majesty without her subjects to praise her and do her biding? What's wrong with using people to obtain your goal if in the process you're uplifting them along the way? Had I not, in a sense, used her for my own purpose? Doesn't our employer, for the company's gain, use not only me but also all the others working there? Hadn't she proven to be a comfort to many, even a guardian angel? Yes! Yes! If anything, that's her redeeming quality, I thought, and that's how I would characterize her.

Hers was housewife-time where bonus spots had been freely logged with any workable contract that had come along, but no more! To the other salesmen, she was no easy sell. Her appeal was a mystery to them because none had followed her programs. They couldn't have understood the way she badgered and put down her listeners, though that kind of mocking was part of her context; it was the way people in this market jested among themselves. I knew all I needed to sell her effectively. For all intents and purposes, her time was mine to sell with no real competition.

I changed gears and cut loose from nurturing the big agencies and went back into the streets. It felt almost like déjà vu of the formative years of my career. But now my motivation was much more than a means to survive. I was polished, unafraid, and going to sell someone that no one else had, someone whose appeal was broadening.

I stepped along the streets on the Westside and the Eastside of Detroit, taking note of the small businesses cropping up. The moment I dropped in on some of these emerging enterprises, I was greeted by Her Majesty's voice coming from the overhead speakers or from small counter radios, and I knew I'd be welcome. It was no contest. The contracts came easily enough, almost like signing autographs. It was a long-awaited labor of love…

…Until a hot, humid summer morning, July 23, 1967.

As people of all colors crowded the streets to escape the heat under their roofs, an early morning police raid on a "blind pig" touched off a chain of reactions on the Westside of the city. Chaos erupted in a hail of rock throwing and looting. Fires fanned by the 25-mile an hour winds burning out of control spread from building to building, enveloping twenty-five blocks. And that went on for days. Police sirens wailed throughout the city. And all night, copters overhead searched the streets for any activity with potent beams of light.

President Johnson sent in federal troops. For several days, volleys of gunfire burst on some of the very streets through which I'd labored. White police and Negroes had often clashed, as they did now in the Algiers Motel executions of three Negroes by white policemen. Everyone knew that the historical culture of the police department viewed Negroes as amoral; and most Negroes saw cops as racist headhunters or worse. So it was not a surprise in the community when police tactics extended to abuse of doctors, lawyers, and in one case, a judge.

The Tower's switchboard was inundated. The station's format was put on hold (though those who didn't comprehend what was going down argued against changing regular programming). Her Majesty's show became a forum through which people were able to express themselves. It was her innate gift to articulate their feelings with her down-home common sense approach to life and its adversities that helped calm some of the fears, especially among people who had only heard the news through the media. At the same time she drew criticism when she zealously chastised callers who thought the whole thing was too long in coming.

I was not surprised the city's structure had been caught off guard completely. No one, least of all the authorities, thought it would happen here. They blamed the "riot" on Black militants. After all, the Motor City – under the leadership of Jerome Cavanaugh, a young, progressive, liberal mayor who had gained much of the people's support – was regarded elsewhere as a model city, one that would do whatever it took to address the long-standing grievances of its citizens.

Clearly, that view from the outside looking in proved terribly wrong. But because they all saw reality through the same comforting lens, the city fathers were unready. Only vaguely had they seen the frustrations of the people, and hardly heard their cries of resentment over personal indignities and police brutality. If they had, they surely wouldn't have been lulled into a false sense of security, expecting a tranquil summer. They could easily have realized that the same symptoms for disruption that broke out in Newark, Watts, and other cities were visible and alive here. They could have discovered that far too many citizens were festering with rage, distrust and contempt for the city's biased system of justice.

In the aftermath, the militants and other political thinkers called it a "rebellion." To prove their case, they cited the founding fathers: "People who are oppressed and can find no other redress must rebel." Some on the streets called it "instant urban renewal." On the other side, the police downplayed it as a "civil disturbance."

Regardless what it was called, the Pandora's box had swung wide open to unleash considerable devastation in parts of the city. More than a thousand families lost their homes, 500 businesses destroyed, 500 or more businesses damaged, 7,231 people of all colors were arrested, 342 injuries, 43 deaths, all at a cost of fifty million dollars in estimated damages. It was determined to be the deadliest and most costly "riot" of the twentieth century.

There was much blame for the "riots" to be spread around. At the top, President Johnson was blamed for putting top priority on the Vietnam War and very little on the problems of the cities. Senator Jacob Javitz called for a kind of Marshall Plan. Governor Otto Kerner, the Chairman of the Riot Commission Report, explained, "The riots in dozens of cities were not caused by hot-eyed hoodlums bent on destruction nor organized conspiracies directed by a revolutionary force that caused the current schism in American life. The causes were ignorance, apathy, poverty, and above all, a pervasive discrimination that has thwarted and embittered the American Negro in every avenue of his life." Most whites, as the news reported, weren't able to buy into those as the causes; they preferred to think that outside agitators and subversive troublemakers were to blame.

The Report further noted that all the "riot" outbreaks were caused by routine arrests of Negroes for minor offenses by white police, and that most of the reported sniping incidents were not from the so-called rioters (as had been widely exaggerated) but were found to be gunfire by police or National Guard.

As for the press, the Report stated, "Along with the country as a whole, the press has too long basked in a white world, looking out of it, if at all, with white men's eyes and a white perspective. Too often the press acts and talks about Negroes as if Negroes do not read the newspapers or watch TV, give birth, marry, die, and go to PTA meetings."

The report echoed what most Negroes knew. They took exception only to its overall conclusion, "This country is moving toward two distinct societies – one Black, one White, separate and unequal." Actually, it did not seem to Negroes that the whole of society was suddenly moving apart. That had already happened centuries before, first in slavery, then under Jim Crow white supremacy and segregation, and finally with de facto segregation, all of which were spirited by institutional racism, the most meticulous form of color discrimination that couched itself in denials, lies, cover-ups and deceit. To the Negro community, the facts were indisputable.

To the mass public, the question became, "What does the Negro want?" Certainly, he wanted equality of opportunity. Better still, as President Johnson said, "Not just equality as a right and a theory, but also equality as a fact and as a result." And yet, a Gallup Poll published July 22, 1967, one day before Detroit's eruption, revealed "Only one white American in 100 thought the Negro was being treated badly." And according to a later study by William Brink and Louis Harris, 85% of whites thought civil rights were moving too fast.

The white press and television, attempting to snare audiences, beat the drums of Black militant violence. They gave a platform to Stokely Carmichal, Rap Brown and other "Black Power" spokesmen who dismissed Dr. King, Whitney Young (of the Urban League) and Roy Wilkinson (of the NAACP) as "Uncle Toms." The militant's attitudes were: We don't hate you, we despise you. We're a nation within a nation. We don't believe in the system. Black folks cannot be concerned about law and order, peace and brotherhood, until we first get justice.

Preachers in the city were asked to urge their congregations to cool it. But Reverend Cleage of the Central United Church of Christ said, "No. We want justice and we are willing to fight for it. The Black community should arm itself to prevent being murdered."

Meanwhile, a New Left radical political movement developed within the white youth counterculture. Their *thang* was "Don't trust anyone over 30!" This period also produced flower children and the anti-war slogan, "Make love not war." But despite the sentiments of their children, many whites grasped for greater repression, and some fled to get away from the cities' problems. In the suburbs, white housewives were learning how to shoot, and the National Rifle Association reported gun sales to civilians reached an all time high.

All of that whirled in an atmosphere of confusion. Polarization was not only between Blacks and whites, but also between Black nationalists and traditional Negroes, and between generations. At this moment in history, the question was not "What does the Negro want?" but whether America would be sustained or if it would be torn by race war or even a hot revolution.

The time of innocence was no more.

CHAPTER NINE

I was restless. I had an urgent need to feel the people's pulse to get a better fix on my city. But where I wanted to go the entire area was blocked off, and there was no word when it would re-open. Frustrated, I resorted to exploring the center of the city's counterculture – the new hippie haven on Plum Street where burning incense filled the air teasing or irritating the nostril. It was one of those dog days in August. The atmosphere was charged with activity and the voices of vendors hawking their wares. As I walked, I lingered at small shops and sought out these people's opinions while I browsed. On this side of town, the Vietnam War was first on everyone's mind, though what I heard were mostly the kinds of sound bytes and catch phrases familiar in the media like "Down with the establishment" and "All power to the people."

Two weeks later, approximately four miles uptown, the wreckage was removed, and the danger zones reopened on Twelfth Street. Under a heavy, eerie stillness, I meandered along the entangled, scattered remnants of the dashed dreams of decimated merchants. This once-popular commercial thoroughfare, where folks from all walks of life had lived, worked, hung out, and played had suffered a multitude of scars because it was the first site where the unrest erupted.

For me, Twelfth Street was undergoing a slow death. But for the cast of characters who were left with nowhere else to go, who'd been conditioned that this was where they'd always congregate and rap, Twelfth Street was the place to be. This was where they could feel the beat and pass it on to others just as the sounds of drums had communicated the very heartbeat of their people over a multitude of generations.

Along some portions of Twelfth Street, seeing the grisly ruins with their darkened, gutted entrails exposed, snuffed out my breath as I remembered what had stood here before. "Soul Brother" signs, now scattered among the rubble, had lent little protection to those businesses. In fact, in some cases, nasty attitudes or jealousy towards the brothers who owned the stores might have targeted those properties for destruction.

My eyes welling with tears, I searched out familiar sites. There was Klein's, a client of mine, where I'd hung out many nights enjoying the music of Yusef Lateep and so many other bands; it's burned-out shell now lurked amidst the destruction. Levin's, the best deli in town – that was gone too.

No one was out on much of Twelfth Street; its color, its gaiety and its passion had disappeared under a precarious calm. In scattered spots, I could still see small groups of men shuckin' and jivin,' talking the same ol' three-six-nine as *the man* rolled slowly by. I was taking it all in. I didn't want to get caught up in anything, only needed to get my bearings on a historical perspective, to feel Twelfth Street's changing beat.

As I neared a crowd in a corner lot, I could hear a speaker's words shoot out like rhythmic reports of an automatic weapon. The rapidity of his rap grabbed me, and I felt compelled to stop just outside the periphery of the crowd.

The speaker's bearded face left only his nose, eyes and forehead uncovered under a decorative kufi hat that crowned his head. Enshrouded in a white African gelaba (a large, flowing caftan), he looked like a mystical black character out of the "Arabian Nights." Though his build was slight, his persona and his rhythmic voice set him apart from the ordinary rapper. He had corralled a sizeable crowd, which prompted a squad car to slow to a stop.

I listened intensely. His rhetoric was not the populist type I'd heard mouthed by seductive politicians; rather it espoused a different kind of beat, a heated, revolutionary beat the likes of which Twelfth Street had never known. On occasion, its profoundness forced me to come up for air and look around, trying to read the others in the crowd.

I could tell a few were uncomfortable by their furtive glances toward the squad car at the curb. Oddly, they unwittingly ignored the paneled truck across the street in which the Red Squad, the city's secret surveillance police unit were capturing us all with their hidden video cameras. I couldn't tell whether the crowd was buying the man's rhetoric; some seemed to hedge towards a loose accord, but I also felt a great deal of skepticism, especially after what they'd just been through.

"Where do you stand on this vital issue?" the speaker challenged. "Are you willing to continue to see your brothers and families destroyed one by one before you resist and take up arms for your own survival? Some say we're crazy—we can't win. That may or may not be true, brothers. Still, you can believe. As an African American, I'm more willing to take the chance of being killed if need be than continue to merely exist—not live—in this racist system of government where you and I are looked upon as nothing. If you're not a relevant part of the Struggle, you're not viable to the solution. So brothers, if you refuse to be programmed any longer, don't procrastinate. Join with us tonight at the African American Brotherhood. Become aware! Hear us in more detail then decide for yourselves."

That night, I hooked up with the group in a small eastside storefront on Mack, and sat bunched with twenty or more others on the floor. The mood was friendly, though we were all aware of the serious undertone. Not used to this kind of setting, wearing my freshly pressed, tight denim jacket, my trousers and posterior were not ready for the hardwood floor.

The window was blocked off. Two flags with bold red, black and green stripes, representing Black liberation, were equally spaced at the front. In the center of each wall, a kerosene lamp burned, lighting the room dimly. Even so, I couldn't help notice, with some disgust, the shameful condition of some heads of hair directly in front of me. When living with Mother Dear, I thought, she wouldn't have allowed me to disgrace her home by going out with my hair in a condition like those – not greased, nappy and matted, beady at the nape of the neck and shapeless. But except for the hair, the dudes looked cool in their striking, colorful dashikis and African robes.

"What time is it?" the bearded one bellowed as he stood up front, towering over us.

"It's Nation time! Nation time! Nation time!" the group chanted back.

The bearded one smiled deeply and raised a clenched fist in a Black Power salute that was echoed by the audience. I hesitated momentarily, undecided if the gesture was for members only, before I followed and raised my fist to the sky. While we held this pose, the bearded one rattled something in Swahili that I couldn't comprehend. That done, he asked each of us in turn to state our name, where we worked and the reason we were present. Most of the adopted names were African and I couldn't have pronounced them if I'd wanted to. I had enough problems remembering names of people I knew, let alone trying to communicate in a totally foreign tongue.

When my turn came, I stated my name, told a little about where I worked, and admitted I'd simply come out of curiosity. That aroused none of the interest that had greeted the African names. I was an outsider. They might even have thought I'd come to spy. In a community rife with police surveillance, you couldn't be sure whom you could trust.

"...If you occupy a people through your pigs, your army and your despicable system," the bearded one intoned, "and you restrict the people's growth and keep them penned up with shame over long periods of time, they become restless and violent. Now, I ask you brothers, where will you be when the revolution comes? Have you stashed your firepower?"

He congratulated those who had taken on African names, then looked over their heads and questioned, "What's in a name?"

A person's name conjures a negative or positive impression of that person, he explained. And the same applies to an entire people. "When a people are stamped with a degrading name," he said, "their image will be degraded."

He moved towards a large box waiting behind him and pushed it forward with his foot. "Let's talk about the name 'Negro,' brothers. The dictionary defines it as referring to people of African descent. But the dictionary neglects to mention the origin – that the name came from Mistuh Charlie and not from the people it was supposed to represent, and that it was created to establish a new strain of African people as beasts of burden."

The speaker continued, "As Brother Malcolm said, 'there's no Negro land, therefore there are no Negro people.' We were African people before we were brought here to be programmed and demonized by Mistuh Charlie. He stamped us with that name after dressing it with everything negative under the sun to humiliate us and destroy our minds to keep us mentally chained in servitude. At the same time, society was infused with Negrophobia in order to make the institution of slavery acceptable. That's why his history doesn't show us as a constructive part. Yet, we all know better. Don't we, brothers?"

The group responded in unison, "Righ'On!" It was the first time I heard that expression. The bearded one drew energy from the consensus, "We helped build this country by the sweat of our balls, but we have very little to show for it. Why? It was all in the planning."

He lifted an armful of placards from the big box and held them on his chest. "Let's check out our minds," he said. "What does the word Negro, as perceived by the majority in this country, bring to your minds?" He allowed the blank placard covering the printed ones to drop into the box.

Together, the group read off each card in strident cadence, as each was uncovered: Inferiority! Shiftlessness! Stupidity! Sneakiness! Irresponsibility! Untrustworthiness! In unison the disciples recited:

"He's a niggah, a monkey, a fool and a thief! If one gets out of control, short of homicide, there's no way of stopping him!"

The leader kicked the box off to his side, and added, with smug sarcasm, "By the way, because of their enormous phalluses, they enjoy raping, especially white women. They enjoy living in slum housing. Keep them out of your neighborhood or your neighborhood will go to pot for being infested with his family and rowdy friends." He paused before continuing, "Now, besides those things," he gave an exaggerated wink, "they're good natured people who've yearned so for the white man's acceptance they've neglected to accept themselves.

"Hear me, brothers. I know what I'm talking about. I was raised as a Negro by a Negro who taught me all she knew as a Negro in Negro-phobic society. *The man* created everything good, heroic and pure in his white image. BULLSHIT! We must continue to let our minds probe deeply within ourselves, searching out all the subliminal messages Mistuh Charlie put down on us. We must pull them up to our consciousness to clearly see them in order to understand the nature of our burden. Then, and only then will we as a people be able to free our own wills and gain our souls, then move on to break free of the mentality of Negro bondage."

He revved towards his conclusion, "No other people who came to this country have had their ethnicity erased to accommodate this society. They are presumed to be Polish Americans, Italian Americans, or whatever their origin." He paused to let his point sink in, and then he called out, "Who are we?"

Quickly and precisely a chorus responded, "We're African American people, black as coal to light cream coffee. Proud! Strong! And determined!"

"Righ'On!" he agreed, "African American people, not Negroes. A Negro is everything we don't want to be. It's Mistuh Charlie's *thang*. Our history as African people goes back to the beginning of mankind on the richest continent on Earth where Jesus walked and performed miracles, where mighty kings ruled and made history long before Mistuh Charlie came crawling out of his cave.

"What time is it?"

"It's Nation time! Nation time! Nation time!" the group chanted.

"Who are we?"

"We're African American people, black as coal to light cream coffee. Proud! Strong! And determined!"

His precise command of the gathering and his astute characterization of the fallacious stereotypes plaguing the Negro were stylistically bracing. This wasn't abstract propaganda. His sarcasm pierced to my soul and struck a responsive chord the way profound truth does when it's brought home.

Of course, this wasn't the first time I'd heard some of these concepts. Malcolm had broken society down to this level of clarity years before, but most people hadn't been ready for his ideas. His album "Malcolm Speaks to the Grassroots" was a gift I'd cherished because it awakened me. I'd played it and a calypso beat by Louis X (later known as Louis Farrakhan), "White Man's Heaven is the Black Man's Hell," for three weeks after Malcolm's death to comprehend the "Black experience" of my forefathers.

But this felt different. I recognized that it was the bearded one's timing, the circumstances under which he appeared, and my state of mind, wanting to become actively involved, that made his rap set so well.

At the end, the audience broke into small groups shaking hands in a symbolic way I hadn't seen before. As I eased towards the exit, I heard my name called out. Turning, I was surprised to see the bearded one himself. I waited warily as he stepped around the groups accompanied by a big, menacing-looking character. He took my hand and shook it in the same strange fashion, punctuating each hand cadence with a word: "Unity. Strength. Power. Self-determination."

He could tell I was not only lost in the handshake, but also new to these ideas. "Don't be embarrassed," he comforted with a disarming, nearly elfin smile. "Take a long hard look at me. In your mind, strip away my beard, cut my hair down some and see what you can see." His hair, like all the others, was greaseless but did have form and some appeal. I examined his face but found it impossible to swipe away his beard. I just couldn't unmask whoever was under it.

The bearded one dismissed the menacing-looking character, "It all right Bulldog. He's cool." Alone with me, he stood loosely, his fingers rubbing lightly over his bearded chin; his head bobbing while his eyes searched mine.

"Think back, little bruh," he chortled, "a long ways back to your childhood in the Gardens, back to a time when the sexiest couple on the screen was Tarzan and Jane. Now I ask who was the hippest and the coolest cat in the Gardens? Who was the baddest dresser, the baddest rugger, the one who could play the dozens for days?" He fell back two steps and turned into a spin. Then he stood tall, his right leg shimmying, and he boasted with a nostalgic smile, "The one the foxes downtown called Swee' Pea."

With the name Swee' Pea and the fluidity of his moves, I was finally able to shave his face. I tried to maintain my cool, as I'd always been taught, but an irrepressible excitement ran through me. My eyes lit up, my mouth popped open in disbelief. I was only nine, and the bearded one seventeen when I last marveled at his old ostentatious flair. Now, as a grown man, a solid citizen, I was standing in awe of him all over again, hardly believing he was the one and only Winston Henry, alias Swee' Pea, but better known to me as Brother Winston, my childhood idol from whom I'd copped much of my street style and finesse.

Seldom had I shown such open affection for a man. I hugged him and patted his back while a kinescope of memories played in my mind. I could picture Winston as a living portrait of rhythmic motion, oozing, gliding, swaggering up to a group of boys who ranged from my age up to fourteen. I could hear his rhythmic greetings, "What the story, Morning Glory? What's the jive y'all cats keepin' alive?" as he tapped lightly on our extended palms before his benediction, "Brother Winston blesses the small-fries. Now your days shall be in harmony with the kings."

I could picture myself as a nine year old sitting quietly; gazing towards the street as if I was oblivious, though I was aware of Winston's every move, and knew soon the jive-talk would begin. I could see the brown cap sitting squarely on his head, his trim body stylishly clothed in corresponding shades from his head to the shiny toes of his Richman's Brothers kicks. I could see him flaunting his obviously manicured and polished nails through the air to his chin, to his belt buckle, and to the crotch of his pants. And I could sense the whiff of spicy cologne that had always been a breath of fragrance among the small fries' musky, sweaty bodies, amidst the mothball smell of our fall sweaters and jackets that hadn't had time to air.

As we moved apart, I wiped the mist of nostalgia from my eyes, and my memories dissolved. He told me he'd kept up with me through the newspapers, that he spotted me in the crowd that morning, and I'd surprised him by showing up at the meeting. He commented that he remembered me as a sharp observer who sat aloof from the other small fries; even then, nothing got past me. I was precocious, he said, and he knew all along I had some smarts. As for him, he was now called Kasuku Mausi. I asked him to repeat that over and over slowly until I pronounced it well.

Kasuku went on to spin a few old yarns, but all the while he spoke, I was trying to recover my bearings. Twenty-eight years had passed, and it was such a contrast to see him now in his exalted revolutionary posture after knowing him only as a hip, easy-going cat whose only claim to fame was good times.

"You've changed your philosophy of life," I said. "Are you for real in all of this?"

"I've never been more serious about anything in my forty-five years. I'm committed to the Struggle," he assured me earnestly. "It's all about jobs, about human dignity, about change, little bruh. Look around at the brothers here. Most of these young dudes believed there was absolutely nothing in life for them. They had nothing to lose, so they came here – the one place they could belong: in the Struggle.

"It's funny how life goes," he smiled remotely. "I've educated myself by reading everything I could get my hands on. As the years went by, I began to see your picture in the *Black Dispatch* and read what you were into. I felt very proud of you." Sincerely, softly, he said, "I'd hoped one day I'd be able to tell you."

"Why didn't you give me a call?"

"I was on the streets. I didn't know if you'd remember me. Besides, I figured I wasn't in your class. You had a good gig. You went to work clean. And you probably hob-nobbed with some of the so-called big boys."

"So what?"

He started to backtrack, to apologize, but I didn't want that. Fascinated, I needed to know what he was trying to accomplish, so even after the others drifted out, I stayed and pressed him to tell me.

He confided, "You know, there was a time after I'd completed my hustle, I'd hang out and celebrate my day. Now, if I'm not on my soapbox, I come here. It doesn't look like much. No lights, no gas, no water, no nothing. But it has spirit. It provides shelter, and it doesn't cost me a dime. I'm building a small army of warriors here."

Privately, I doubted how viable his army was likely to be, counting the twenty or so I'd seen tonight. But I nodded so he'd keep going, wanting to understand.

"Take Bulldog for instance," he waved towards the brute still watching from the side. "He's my strong-arm lieutenant, big and threatening looking. Because of my size, some dudes think they can run over me, at first. But with Bulldog at my side, those thoughts quickly fade."

"I know that's right," I smiled.

"Everything we do is geared to building discipline and self worth through a process of deprogramming that few brothers are aware of. Hey, little bruh," he emphasized with a shrug, "If people don't know who they are, they act out what they think they're supposed to be.

"Our handshake adds real meaning to our Struggle and speaks to what we're all about. It spells out revolution and self-determination, a new way of thinking, a new way of building people-power and a nation. We raise our clenched fist in celebration of our liberation. We express ourselves differently."

He was gaining steam, building up to the rhetoric I'd already heard. When he paused for a breath I asked, "Like 'Righ'On,?" still trying to appreciate the scene.

Eagerly, he went with that. "We don't say Amen like the old folks. We say Righ'On because it's youthful and vigorous. There's no CPT here. The brothers get here on time, and we start on time. They sit on the floor in silence unless they're asked to speak. I've seen real growth in these brothers, especially Bulldog. They're orderly, clean, and non-threatening unless provoked, and now all of them have disciplined minds."

I couldn't help agreeing that "CPT," colored people's time, which meant always being late, was a sloppy habit, and if he could give some of these brothers a hint of the mental discipline I'd learned early at home, they'd have a chance at whatever they wanted to do. But taking up guns and waging revolution was another matter.

At first he played it off, low, "Hey, I just say that for shock value, to let Mistuh Charlie know we mean business." Still, he couldn't let go of the idea, as his voice rose. " But if things don't change soon for the better in this country, a hot revolution really will be coming. I personally hope that time never comes, but we got to be ready. And you, little bruh, won't be able to hide behind your nice position or your nice looks. Remember that we all act and look alike to them. You'll be drawn into it whether you want to or not."

He glared a challenge straight into my eyes: "Where will you be when the revolution comes? Will you have firepower? Or will you run for cover and hide your greasy head?"

CHAPTER TEN

The talk of guns and revolution had taken the sheen off my reunion. Back at my crib, I contemplated in silence, blaming guns for the world's ills because being armed gave cowardly men a sense of bravado that pushed far too many to tragic consequences.

Had I not served in Korea, I doubt I would have ever known the sensation of arming myself. I would not have risked playing God with someone else's life the way I did one cold night in no-man's-land when I experienced that awful, frightening rush of anxiety that beset me while I fired tracers at the shadowy images of a groping enemy patrol. No – guns were not part of me. I'd have to pass on Kasuku's clarion call to arms.

But then I wondered what Kasuku really meant by his talk of revolution. Up to a point, I understood the mental revolution – but a hot one? I'd always thought my gig had strengthened my understanding of my market. How had any part of my market gotten so completely out of my grasp? I'd managed to balance my life successfully between two distinct worlds. But had my drive to get ahead made me callous to my very own surroundings? Had my social ambience limited my perceptions so that my meticulous discernment of my market was pushed to the background of my all-assuming little world?

Then something mystical happened. My thinking machine

conked out, leaving me in limbo, holding back any answers. I did know this much: I'd forever treasure the memories of that afternoon and night as the quintessential performance of my childhood idol. Kasuku's tour de force had sensitized me beyond my wildest expectations.

I became obsessed with a thirst to keep growing by enriching my mind. Reluctantly, I brought Bonner up to date on business at hand, and then took time off to find out more. On my quest I traveled to five major cities to participate in forums, workshops, lectures and to brainstorm at conferences centered on Black economics, Black political power and Black attitudes.

But to claim my market was as eager as I was in its struggle to embrace "Blackness" would be a gross overstatement. The "whole mess" confused people of Mother Dear's generation. They couldn't understand the burnings, the killings, the nappy heads and the ugly term "Black." They were simply thankful God had blessed them and their families to come so far with so little. After all, it was less than three decades ago when they'd won the battle to have Mrs. or Mr. before their names, as the result of their efforts with the Urban League.

Some preferred to be called colored because their complexions came in various shades. Others preferred Negro because that capital N had been hard-won in their struggle for society's respect, and they believed making it a proper noun made them a people.

And then there was opposition from Negroes who'd inherited fair complexions and straight hair, who'd been indoctrinated since birth with a sense of being in a class of their own. Wanting to be white or similar to whites, they were adamantly against being labeled Black. The fear ran deep that they'd be deprived of the special privileges that society bestowed on the offspring of the master, since the days of slavery. If they lost their mystique (similar to the position blue-eyed blondes hold in white society) they'd no longer be able to look down their noses on their darker brothers and sisters, and there status – in fact, their entire subculture—would crumble. The general consensus of the cats on the street was "They think their shit don't stink!"

To this class of Negroes, the media's take on the movement was correct: Black militancy was something to fear, something to reject the same way that some house-slaves who, for fear of their master's disaffection, distanced themselves from their sisters and brothers in the field. Within them there seemed to exist a self-hatred toward their color, and that alone proved they had a "slave mentality" that inhibited them from accepting anything as certain unless sanctioned first by whites. To be called Black was nearly as demeaning to them as being called a nigger.

Others were taking up the question seriously, and I discerned three schools of thought. The integrationist would give up his Black culture in order to blend into white institutions and their mindset. The separatist pressed for a voluntary physical and cultural separation from whites and urged Blacks to build upon the cultural base of their forefathers. The liberationist would disregard the white man and dismiss the society that had been built around the ostensibly moral and intellectual superiority of the white man, and develop a new political entity inhabited entirely by strong-minded, unified Blacks, along the lines Malcolm preached.

Everywhere I traveled, "Nation Time!" was the prevailing idea. That meant it was time for Blacks to repudiate the National Anthem and honor their own because Black Americans were not respected enough to be given the same basic civil rights as white Americans. It was imperative for Blacks to document their own history and form closer ties with their African brothers who were in a similar Struggle. It was imperative for Blacks to determine their own destiny and their own place in this society by defining their own image, their own art, their own culture, and their own conception of beauty, their own heroes, their own religion and politics. It was imperative for Blacks to halt the disruptive police violations set upon their communities, and to disallow the white press into their meetings. What's more, they must no longer allow the system to hand-pick their leaders, nor be beguiled by "handkerchief-head Negroes," whose purpose was to impose the white man's will and thinking on Blacks.

In the three weeks I'd taken off, I discovered that all the cities were like my own. Across the board, neighborhoods and churches were segregated, politics were segregated in reality if not in principle, and while some schools were partially integrated, the social activities within them usually were not.

All the while, I gained perspective on myself. I'd gone through a metamorphosis, and now I was a whole man, energized and armed with the truth, prouder than ever before. In my mind, I'd gone over the hump to liberation. Any traces of subliminal confusion, shame or misgivings that may have crept into my psyche were completely expelled like a laxative flushing filth from the system. At last, I was deprogrammed and truly understood the issue of "Blackness." It was an attitude, a state of mind, a change from the traditional values held by many in the mainstream who thought of themselves as superior to Blacks.

In Black communities across the country, a schism had opened between those of the "slave mentality" who sought white approval, and those of the "revolutionary concept," who sought self-approval. Even so, I was convinced that when my market found its elusive bond – when the schism healed – the Black community would finally emerge as a power in both its economic and political force, through its unified vote.

So I trashed the mask I'd worn all these years and displayed a new attitude, determined to take command of my feelings and assert my true self.

When I returned to The Tower, I shared my experience with Her Majesty, but she was not impressed. Her eyes told the story as they strayed back and forth from the Afro I'd nurtured and groomed with meticulous care to the commercial material at her side. Like many Negroes, she frowned on Afros and Blacks wearing African dress or learning Swahili. She couldn't grasp the "mental revolution" that was arising, nor why I was indulging in the ideology of "Blackness," which, to her, was a waste of time.

I should have expected her response. Like others who shared her lighter hue, she was color-struck too. On the air, even though she tried to sound neutral whenever the subject arose, invariably she became flustered and created differences with callers in her audience, or she faltered so awkwardly she would have to regroup. That took its toll as her show lost much of its appeal and her audience was crumbling, as was her pedestal. She became hopelessly at odds with herself. Now she'd need to pull herself together and find a way to recapture some of her previous celebrity and regain the audience she once commanded. She still had the talent and the tool to do it, but she'd have to find a new way to wield it.

After the riots, many agencies left the city for the surrounding suburbs. Nevertheless, the industry was turning in my direction. While the major advertisers used to write off non-whites and cater primarily to the white majority, now, because of the polarization between whites and blacks, their attitudes had to change. Integrated advertising was born.

This turn-around prompted me to try to make an even bigger impact on their frame of reference. In my judgment, the advertising industry and the media were the umbilical chords that fed most consumers' minds. I wanted to encourage both advertisers and broadcasters to digest the new image of my market. So I collaborated with one of my close friends in public relations and designed a classy, eight-page brochure to send the agencies and media outlets to whet their appetites.

The brochure was titled "Some Frank Facts about Old Attitudes and the New Negro Market." Within were my business, civic and community affiliations, my credentials, and graphic layouts showing the growth of my market's income, along with population figures from 1940 up to projections for 1975. Subtitles in bold print included: New Advertisers' Attitudes, the Key to Successful Negro Market Appeal; Management's Attitudes toward Negro Employees Need Changing; The New Responsibilities of Agencies and the Black Man's New Self Image – all discussed within. The brochure ended with my phone number and a statement giving my deepest thanks and best wishes to both Black and white individuals and firms who'd helped me reach my understanding and position.

I then prepared my presentation step by step. It was all about attitudes, I reasoned – those embedded sentiments, which continued to preclude my city and the surrounding suburbs from coming together. I had to prick beneath the consciousness where many of these sentiments were harbored without being harsh or intimidating, and without emphasizing "Blackness" too firmly, for it could be frightening and a turn-off for the naive. Of more than 750 brochures I'd sent out using mailing lists from Adcraft, the City, and several of my business affiliates, I received an eight percent return, which was more than enough. After several weeks I'd gotten appointments with all of them.

With a renewed sense of urgency, I hit the agencies and the media. Using my experiences with Kasuku and what I'd recently gained from my travels, I blended highlights of those viewpoints with my own style. Shock was eliminated. I exploited the strengths of knowledge, sincerity, salesmanship, and appearance. My crusade succeeded in stirring the big ad agencies to take another look at the viability of my market as a reasonable buy, and I took solace that I had heralded my market's new image, and had put the anxieties of some potential clients at ease. Only a few were left with polite indifference and sour faces.

As this revolutionary time went on, the "Struggle," as I now called it, had taken a toll on The Tower. Bonner was in serious trouble. The community's reticent temperament had changed. People no longer cloaked their feelings to suit society's expectations as they'd been taught. Relief was necessary; the people said so loudly, and in public.

For a long time, one source of discontent was the jack-legged preachers. Those programs sparked numerous protest calls to The Tower, badgering Bonner, straining his nerves. He'd already lost several of those preachers, and the sales department had lost multiple accounts. For the sake of his job, he couldn't afford to lose any more business. He was in dire straits, needing an escape. So he called Karl to his office, placed the responsibility in his lap, and then took off on an unscheduled vacation.

Karl, in charge, had no intention of taking his livelihood off the air. He refused to respond to the complaining call-ins. Beverly, the phone operator, didn't know what to do, so she transferred those calls to me, believing I could handle the crisis. But I had no power to satisfy the protests.

I called Butler, who promised to call back, but an hour passed, then another hour, as I grew increasingly frustrated. I knew the dilatory pace at The Buhl, and I imagined Butler sitting around, doing nothing while he ignored the call back he'd promised. The image whipped me into action. If nothing else, I wanted Butler to feel the brunt of the problem first hand, so I asked Beverly to send the call-ins directly to him.

As expected, Butler soon phoned me, pleading, "Stop the calls! Stop the calls!" I agreed only if he'd tell Karl to take them. Butler refused, wanting nothing to do with Karl. "You do it," he said. I agreed with one stipulation – that for the benefit of the company he and I would meet at our usual place.

Three other salesmen overheard all that. Throughout, Karl rocked in his seat, stirring in sullen silence at the back of my neck. He'd overheard me taking the call-ins. That, he didn't mind. But to direct the calls to Butler was an affront that made him look small. When I hung up, Karl had the audacity to jump up and get in my face.

"Who gave you the authority to send the call-ins to Butler?"

I answered calmly, "That was my decision. Why?"

"You should've checked with me before you did it!" Karl insisted.

"Check with you for what? If you had been on the case neither Butler nor I would've been involved."

Tempers flared and we got into a verbal skirmish, which the others pretended not to notice. Realizing the tussle wasn't going anywhere, I said, "You're blocking my path, man—back off, fool!"

But Karl stood his ground. I rose to make my point clear, to take an action that had tempted me for a long, long time. I rammed my chair against Karl's knees. Karl buckled and stumbled back over the carpet and on to the floor. The three salesmen no longer could avoid looking on in amazement at my actions that belied the cool I'd usually displayed in the past.

Determined to expose the true caliber of The Tower's leadership, I told Beverly to direct all the complaints back to Karl, and to tell her relief operator to do the same. "Feed him regardless of what he says." Beverly blinked in bewilderment. "That's an order from Butler," I reinforced the point, and then left.

Fifteen minutes later, I rendezvoused with Butler. I explained that Bonner was irresponsible for going away under these circumstances, and Karl should not have been left in charge. Neither was capable of performing their jobs, and I could no longer conduct my business while responding to the complaints. I wouldn't even have gotten involved except that I was concerned about satisfying my community. I strongly suggested Butler get engaged before The Tower really experienced the community's backlash.

Unaware of the entire situation until now, Butler immediately went to the pay phone and tried to locate Bonner, to no avail. He returned upset, and confessed I was right about Karl. Karl was the rat who'd informed Bonner about the occurrence at the Christmas luncheon (Butler's embarrassing tryst with the prostitutes). Because of that, Butler had cut off all communication with Karl. He asked if I'd be his contact, and revealed, "If I had the right people to replace them, I would've had Mr. Beck fire both long ago."

"May I suggest a way of getting rid of Karl and replacing him with the right person?" I asked. Butler nodded, and I pressed my point: "Take those jack-legged preachers off the air. It's as simple as that. Karl will have no business left to sustain him unless by some miracle he gets to understand the market over night and learns how to sell it. As for Bonner, I don't have any suggestions, though."

Butler implied that he might have one, if I was willing to back him up. He offered to talk more about it later, and Mr. Beck would have to settle this when he got back in town. He closed by asking me to do whatever I saw fit to keep things under control. I shrugged and left.

I'd never seen so much fudging on an issue. What could I do? Even if I scratched the programs off the log, that wouldn't stop anything without the engineers' cooperation, and I doubted they'd put their jobs at risk for me. I wasn't surprised by Karl's actions, but for the captain to bail out of his teetering ship was something else. One thing was for sure: If there was any truth in what Butler hinted, Bonner wouldn't be a problem for long.

On my return to The Tower, I found the ladies steaming over Karl's maneuver – he'd left shortly after me, dumping the call-ins on the receptionists. I calmed them by assuming the responsibility, and luckily, the barrage had tapered off. I could do no more for now. I'd have to press on until I had the upper hand to do my community's will.

When Bonner returned, the jack-legged preachers were still airing because they were a source of revenue. Though they were an insult to my community, Mr. Beck didn't personally feel the indignity or the need to take them off.

The questions raised were: What were Bonner and Karl's excuses for disregarding their duties? Why had they abandoned their watch? Bonner insisted he'd been called out of town on an emergency because a very close relative was on his deathbed. Karl's alibi sounded somewhat honest, admitting he'd been overwhelmed in a perplexing situation. Regardless, everyone knew why both had taken flight, and it was apparent that neither measured up to the challenge. The ladies made that crystal clear. Their lack of guts fostered contemptuous undertones throughout the staff with implications that impugned their ability to lead.

In contrast, I'd captured the energy and admiration of most of my co-workers, so my goal had been accomplished. And while this incident was only the beginning of taking actions towards my new resolve, I was now guardedly optimistic about the future and my ambition.

As the storm was passing, Martin Luther King was assassinated. His death cast a long shadow over the entire country, and some cities erupted in violence. In Detroit, the mood in the community was somber, and fortunately, the streets were manageable. Maybe the Detroit Tigers winning the '68 World Series had something to do with keeping things settled. Still, Black America died a little. To many people of color, the assassination meant we had no hope. With no one to take Dr. King's place, his non-violent movement lost its champion, and of course, people believed white America was responsible.

In the shadow of King's death, coming at the very point when the Black Consciousness Movement was coalescing, myriad all-Black groups formed throughout the country – on college campuses, in professional associations of social workers and teachers, and in Black political and social action organizations. The most visible world-wide expression was at the 1968 Olympics as the American flag waved in the breeze and the Star Spangled Banner played, when Tommy Smith and John Carlos saluted the flag by raising their gloved clenched fists in Black protest.

Of all the efforts keeping the community together, Black radio was foremost. Amidst desolation, nothing pulled people's spirits up from the pervasive malaise of impotence more than its music that spoke to its heart. Black radio was the primary means of sharing the market's soul. From its play list came the uplifting lyrics of celebrated artists, among whom none echoed the times better than James Brown and Aretha Franklin. Their voices fortified the psyche of the community and incited people to sing out loud and clear to James' "Say it Loud! I'm Black and I'm Proud!" and to Aretha's expression of "Respect."

In this ferment, Detroit got its first Black TV news anchorman, and the city became one of the vanguards of the Black Struggle. The Republic of New Africa, a disciplined Black legion, based in Detroit, which claimed to speak for three million Blacks nationally, was seeking reparations for Black folks' centuries long suffering, in addition to laying claim on five Southern states. Though outsiders did not take its position seriously, it was attracting Blacks who had given up on the move toward assimilation and were now concerned only with Black solidarity, which would lead to their control of their community.

Black people questioned information that they'd previously accepted on faith. Who really wrote the Bible? What was the complexion of Jesus? Why were there no Blacks in the hierarchies of major religious denominations? Why were there no Black movie roles besides buffoons and Beulahs? Why were there no Black dolls, no mannequins, no models, and certainly no Black Miss America?

It all became too clear: The "Man" made it seem that everything good, heroic and pure was in his image. He's God, he's Jesus, he's Santa Claus, and he's Tarzan, King of the African jungle! "Bullshit" echoed the brothers on the streets.

But in any revolution the good comes along with the bad. I could plainly see the bad: In parts of my market drugs were now evident along with methadone clinics. And the cry for security led to burglar alarm systems, steel gates, steel doors, and steel window guards in homes, and protective Plexiglass and rent-a-cops in our stores. The camaraderie I'd once experienced on some streets had all but dissipated. The streets were no longer the place to be, to lollygag and feel their beats. The rogue elements were now in charge, lost in a deadly game of dope.

Meanwhile, Her Majesty aligned herself with the Police Commissioner as hostess of the "Buzz the Fuzz" show whose intent was to help bring the police and the community together. Though the city establishment touted it, it was a dismal flop in the Black community, which felt Her Majesty was kowtowing to the Commissioner.

As a matter or survival, she hurriedly came up with a strategy she felt would suit her character. With her rustic, down-home savvy, she resorted to a religious bag and brought her pulpit to the air. "In my bleakest hour," she said, "God spoke to me and told me to go forth and take His words to the people!"

Her preparation was weak at best—she seemed to have gone on her feelings alone. Hardly a day passed without her getting into a scrape with a call-in who knew the Bible far better. While proclaiming to be a messenger of God, she couldn't bear criticism. If a caller gave the least inkling critical of her interpretation, she would proceed to humiliate him, firing off snide remarks and zapping his line before he had a chance to make his point clear. Of course, that was not the type of manners thought to be proper for a spiritual leader, much less a lady.

As time went on, she began to study with a few scriptural scholars, attending retreats and engaging in serious homework until she emerged anew on the air as if one of God' prophets. Now she had something of worth to share that took the onus off her and placed it squarely on God's words. She was home free. No one but the devil's advocates would dare argue with the unvarnished truth. And if they did, she no longer humiliated them; she merely pulled the plug.

During the course of her transition I saw her through two perspectives. I still loved and needed her for my purposes, despite her capricious behavior. And yet we were estranged since she supported Bonner because he allowed her to do whatever she pleased. Even though we weren't in sync about Bonner, I believed I could bring her into the fold. To accomplish this, I first needed to fabricate a scenario…

I called Butler and shared part of my plan. Then I called Donald Lacey. I wanted to know if his attitude about WDDD had changed. Lacey said it hadn't – he was still unhappy there – and that encouraged me to try enticing Lacey to The Tower. I suggested he meet with Butler and me for drinks at the Tender Trap, a strip club in Highland Park, a small city within Detroit where I'd entertained a few special male clients. However, unknown to Lacey and Butler, I had a whole concoction in mind. I figured if Lacey came in as sales director, Bonner could be squeezed out later and Lacey would take on Bonner's position and I would take over sales. On top of that, because of the bad blood between Lacey and Her Majesty, I gambled on using Lacey as a pawn to force her back in my good graces; she'd need me on her side.

I picked up Butler that evening and headed to the Tender Trap. Lacey was there already enjoying the lewd entertainment. The minute Butler stepped in and eyed the nude stripper bumping and grinding around the horseshoe bar, he was blown away. I purposely hadn't told him about the nature of the bar to catch him off guard and stir up his jollies.

We were seated. After ordering drinks from the topless waitress, I spelled out to Lacey what Butler and I had in mind. As I'd anticipated, it soon became my show, for Butler's attention wasn't at the table but on the ladies on stage. Lacey was disclosed his first priority: dump the jack-legged preachers and bring the sales department together. Lacey only wanted to know what kind of time frame we were looking at. I turned to Butler. But seeing him still preoccupied, I said, "That's up to Butler, but I'd guess a month or more. I'll keep you posted." And I told him not to divulge this meeting to anyone.

Satisfied, we joined Butler. As the two of them watched the ladies' performance, I was watching Butler and Lacey, glad they were hitting if off nicely. Lacey volunteered to drive Butler back to his office since I had another stop, and I left while they were having a blast. Now that one part of my plan was in place, I was ready to attend to others.

Winding down at my crib that night, I became caught up in sober reflection over my relationship with Kasuku. I'd been avoiding his calls, but only because my schedule had been so tight. I needed time to spare whenever we kicked it. And while our styles, attitudes and approaches to life were different, we'd both come to respect each other's intelligence and understood where the other was coming from in the Struggle.

Kasuku saw me as a well-connected brother who could pull strings and move through the establishment he was fighting, though he realized I had neither the fire in my belly or the inclination to become a real revolutionary. Meanwhile, I saw Kasuku as a committed brother with a misguided approach that could lead him to a dead end. Nevertheless, every time we met, each of us always tried to convert the other, and while our talks were energizing, they were also endless. Still, I needed to touch base with him now.

The following day, I hooked up with Kasuku at his den on Mack. We revisited old times in the Gardens and had some good hearty laughs about some of its characters. As time moved on, weak with laughter, we paused for a breath. I had some impressions of what was going down on the streets and asked Kasuku what he was seeing. His mood quickly changed. He explained there was a panic on the streets created by Mistuh Charlie who'd dried up the pot and gotten small gangs flooding the streets with scag. On the streets, people were speculating that the CIA or one of those secret government operatives were in collusion with the pigs and the Mafia to kill off the revolution by filling the brothers' veins with that shit. I wanted to know what proof he had. But Kasuku became agitated, offended I'd question what he knew.

He admitted he couldn't prove his accusations, but wanted me to think on this: Who else could create this type of panic throughout the community? Who else had the money and the facilities to grow, process, import, and distribute that shit free? He doubted it could be the po' brothers 'cause they don't have a pot to piss in or a window to throw it out. The ploy was to get the bloods hooked, and charge them afterward for more. Charlie knew damn well that with more than thirty percent of the young brothers unemployed they wouldn't be able to pay the freight.

"Where do you suspect they'll get the bread to supply their habits?" Kasuku challenged. "The bloods will get so desperate for the shit they'll rip off you, rip off me, and rip off anyone else to feed their veins." He expounded on other eventualities and wanted me to use my influence to get him on the air so he could pull the people's coats.

He'd gotten my attention, alarming me by the weight of his tone. I found myself sitting there giving the matter real thought. Not that I doubted Kasuku or that I was attempting to decide if I should help, but only trying to fathom the matter's earthshaking gravity. In the end, Kasuku's theories, though plausible, were too much of a stretch. Without proof I couldn't accommodate him. The Tower's management wouldn't dare touch it and neither would the jocks.

But I didn't want to leave Kasuku seeing me the way he saw all the other established Black men—impersonal and hardly listening to what was going on. So I told him where my head was, that I agreed with the detrimental effects of the drugs on the street. And I shared what I had in mind for the future – an agenda much to Kasuku's liking. Once he heard my plan, Kasuku swore to be at my side with his warriors whenever he got the call.

CHAPTER ELEVEN

Her Majesty had left a message to come to her office. Whenever she asked to see me, something had gone awry, so I wasn't surprised to find her so angry she couldn't concentrate on the pile of work in front of her. Her small office was cramped and cluttered with knickknacks. Framed awards hung on the walls, but her favorite image was a freshly made portrait of her that captured the spiritual, regal prominence for which she had longed. Her hair was adorned with a light blue turban that matched her flowing robe, and she towered majestically against a pale blue sky as if she had emerged up out of the earth.

I squeezed around her desk to the chair facing her, and tried to lighten the mood, "Hey lady, what's up?"

She inquired if I'd heard anything about Donald Lacey coming to the station.

"No, what's the deal?"

Simmering, she said she'd gotten word from a good source that said that he and Lacey were bending elbows when Lacey told him he'd been talking to the people here, and that he'll be coming in to take over sales. "If that's true," she said, "why him and not you? You know the market. Plus, you're a much better salesman than him."

Of course, I couldn't argue with her points, but I told her I wouldn't be surprised if what she'd heard was true. As for why – I surmised it was the plantation mentality of Mr. Beck, who believed Blacks were inherently unqualified to lead because of their supposed inferior intellectual character.

"But don't that bother you, child?" she said.

I knew the attitude at The Buhl and it didn't matter because I understood the game well enough to play it my way as long as playing it served my purpose. So I answered, "No. And I haven't heard anything, but if it's true, I'm not going to lose any sleep. Lacey and I can respect one another."

"Huh! You think you know Lacey, but you don't. That son of a bitch ain't about nothing! He's an opportunist! He's the biggest liar! He plays games! He's a manipulator – or at least he attempts to be."

"And Bonner's not?" I probed.

She shook her head and argued that he's a good man, very sensitive, who tries to be fair and does his best to get along with everybody. Then she said, "He told me about your attitude toward him. Plus, he told me if you don't change your ways he'd have no choice but to let you go. He thinks you hate him. What's happening, child?"

I chuckled. None of what she said was relevant to me, but I knew she wouldn't be able to understand. It wasn't about hate. I'd come to realize hate was a negative energy that restricted my thinking and brought more turbulence to me than to my foe. But if I'd tried to explain, she'd put it down as more of my mumbo jumbo. So I answered, "No, I don't hate the man. I'm disappointed in him, I distrust him, and therefore, I disregard him."

"Ah c'mon, child, isn't there anything nice you can say about him?"

I smiled, remembering the words of Mother Dear: "If you can't speak truthfully from the heart, don't speak." There was nothing I could say except that she was cozy with the man. And she should've gone to Bonner instead of me to put her mind at ease about Lacey.

Her Majesty countered, "I did, but he knows nothing." Then she assured me that she wasn't worried about herself – her concern was on my behalf. But if I wasn't worried, neither was she. As I rose to leave, she bet me that if Lacey came, I'd be up in arms about him mighty quick, and don't say she didn't warn me.

I blew a kiss her way, thanked her, and reminded her that in spite of our differences I still loved her.

But as I headed for my office I was steaming over Lacey's broken promise to keep our secret, going to jump on the phone with him, when Bonner spotted me. To my surprise, Bonner smiled and asked if I had a minute. He said he wanted to talk over some things and wondered if I had time for coffee. I didn't see myself sitting down to coffee with this man, but when Bonner asked me for just a few minutes in his office, I reluctantly accompanied him, though Lacey was still crowding my thoughts.

Bonner sat and smoothed over his desk pad, groping for the right approach. His hair and his physical stature had diminished so he was nothing but a caricature of the man I'd first met. It had been such a long time since we'd last talked that Bonner hardly knew where to begin. I made no effort to ease the way. I lit up a smoke, curious to see how Bonner would recover. Finally, he apologized and confessed that he had wanted to sit with me for some time but his pride wouldn't allow him. He'd hoped to start the sales meetings again but was reluctant for fear I wouldn't participate. In fact, he had the feeling I was trying to get back at him for some unknown reason.

I couldn't help a slight smirk as I thought what a crock.

Bonner said he was deeply wounded when I took that swipe at him at our last meeting. He still didn't know why it happened. Even so, he told me he was putting his pride aside to ask for my participation, "Sales needs your input."

I understood that. I also understood that I was the only one in sales who lived, worked, played and worshipped in my market yet my candid opinions about the market's sentiments fell on deaf ears most times. That, among other problems, were why I brought the meetings to an abrupt end. Nevertheless, it was good to finally hear Bonner admit for the first time that what I'd brought to the table had some merit. Still, that wasn't enough.

I said, "I was under the impression that sales meetings were held to benefit everyone. Yet I found myself always giving, never receiving. Plus, most of what I said didn't seem to arouse any interest or understanding. So what purpose would my presence serve?"

"I don't know why you had that impression. We all looked forward to learning what you would say about the market."

Secure enough in my position and determined to show no mercy, I retorted, "Mr. Bonner, one learns by doing it. And no one else here was doing it. No, I'm not interested in wasting any more of my time."

I felt a little gratification as I hurried to my office. I picked up the receiver to contact Lacey, but set it back in place. I was comfortable with Her Majesty's disclosure and decided to deal with Lacey's word as something to be watched closely. I'd let the matter slide. My plan was coming together and the time was too near to risk any friction.

But I didn't know yet that Lacey was already plotting my downfall. He perceived that Butler and I had a good relationship, but didn't know to what extent. He also knew Butler's standing at The Buhl and wanted to get between Butler and me in order to deal above me at the top. So he snooped around for personal information from someone who knew Butler's family well. As it turned out, that person happened to be the very source that informed Her Majesty about Lacey coming to The Tower.

Lacey learned that his wife who wouldn't allow him out of her sight when he returned from work henpecked Butler. Anything he wanted to indulge had to be accomplished before he got home. That probably explained how he acted toward his subordinates at The Buhl. With what he uncovered about Butler together with what he'd witnessed directly at the bar, Lacey knew Butler was weak for the ladies. And that fit well into his plan. He made his move. He invited Butler to be his guest for drinks at The Tender Trap. It didn't take much persuasion – Butler was ready. And, as Lacey expected, Butler was easily seduced by the excitement, so much that it became a weekly event.

During the same time, I tried to keep in touch with Lacey, as promised, but I couldn't catch him at work. I left messages, but he never called back. Under the circumstances, that seemed strange, and I wondered what was happening. Finally, I reached Cathy, who assisted Butler in making out the commission sheets. That's when I put it all together, when Cathy unwittingly revealed that Butler had been leaving early for the past several weeks.

Were they meeting together and didn't want me to know? Were they trying to undermine me in my very own scheme? Was that why Lacey refused to return my calls? If so, I'd better stay ahead of the curve.

Cathy was not only Butler's assistant; she was also my friend. We'd struck up a relationship while checking my commission sheets after I'd found errors. She didn't think well of Butler but to keep her job she pretended to respect his position. Sometimes when she was at low ebb, my calls had lifted her spirits. Now I needed someone who was cognizant of Butler's movements to keep me abreast. So I asked Cathy if she would check with me the next time Butler took off, and she was more than happy to help me.

I stayed close to my office, prepared to make my move at a moment's notice. It wasn't long before Cathy called alerting me that Butler was leaving to meet someone downstairs. It was pure speculation on my part, but if I was correct, and I hurried, I'd beat them to their haunt.

Twenty minutes later I pulled up in the parking lot behind The Tender Trap. Entering through the back door, I looked over the crowd. The set hadn't begun and the two hadn't arrived. I sat at a table in the shadows that afforded me a perfect view of the front door and the area where I expected they'd sit. I ordered a martini, and waited. Ten minutes passed. They should've been here by now, I thought. I wondered if my theory was faulty, and if so, where could they be. Before I could finish my thought, there they were – the two of them coming in like exuberant teenagers out for a night on the town.

They sat at the curve of the bar, their backs to me. I observed them for a while. From their body language, they appeared to be in some kind of disagreement. I wondered whether I should let them see me, or leave without them knowing I was there. I decided that their reaction to seeing me would reveal whether my suspicions were correct. I swallowed my drink, moved behind them, and touched each on his shoulder. As both turned and faced me, complete shock registered on their faces. Recovering, they had no choice but to ask me to join them. I begged off, saying my client and I had seen the first show and I had business to take care of back at The Tower. But my suspicion was validated. As I left I wondered if Lacey suspected what was up my sleeve.

It was some time later that I found out Lacey was poisoning Butler against me at the bar that night, claiming he'd heard I was a Black militant and a member of organizations such as the Black Panther Party. All those accusations disturbed Butler greatly, and relief from Lacey's diatribe only came when the show kicked off and grabbed their attention.

The following day, Butler was filled with consternation over what he'd heard. He didn't want to believe it, but Lacey was persuasive. He had to get some kind of verification. Believing his relationship with me was up-front, he asked me to meet at our usual place. There, he repeated what he'd heard and asked straight out if any of it was true.

I answered that it was another "he said, she said," and wanted to know who had put out those lies, and if my accuser knew me well enough to know what I did outside the job? Butler wouldn't tell, though he indicated the person knew me and was very convincing. I listened intensely to pick up any clues, while questions popped in my head. Who was close enough to know my activities? Outside The Tower, with the exception of some jocks, I hadn't socialized with anyone but Butler. And who at The Tower was tight enough with Butler to share that kind of information?

I explained to Butler that I was acquainted with many so-called Black militants and had attended some of their meetings to stay up on that part of my market; however, I wasn't one of them. I looked Butler straight in the eye and let him know that among other things I was a business, social and community activist who belonged to a number of clubs and business associations. I pulled a couple of napkins from the dispenser, wiped over a section of the table, unlatched my attaché case that rested beside me in the booth, removed a small pouch of cards and spread them face up on the table. I asked Butler if he recognized any of the names. Butler was familiar only with The Detroit Chamber of Commerce, New Detroit, Inc., The Adcraft Club of Detroit, and the NAACP – four of the nine. I pointed out that the others were business associations composed of Black-marketing specialists from all over the country. I suggested that Butler pick any or all of the others and I would give him the information he needed in case he wanted to make inquiries there. Of course, Butler wasn't up to going fishing. He waved off the offer, saying he didn't believe my accuser in the first place.

I remembered the body language I'd observed between Lacey and Butler at The Tender Trap. Before today Butler had never asked about my feelings towards Black militants or the Panthers. I smiled as the identity of the betrayer came alive: It could only be Lacey, and I remarked on realizing the extent that Lacey would prevaricate to suit his purpose. Still, Butler didn't understand how I'd figured it out.

"It was easy," I said. "He probably used The Tender Trap to prey on your weakness."

Confronted by that reality, Butler could only ask why I'd bring that type of person to him. It was the good things I'd said about Lacey that had encouraged him to go along.

Actually, I couldn't afford to lose Lacey at this point, so I said, "Don't pay much mind to what he attempted to do. I suppose he was just trying to get on your good side and push me out of the mix." I advised him to go along and pretend I was no longer part of the deal, and in fact to make Lacey accountable only to him, to keep him on a short leash, just enough to see to what extent he'd try to go. Though Butler still didn't understand, I cautioned him to stay the course. The important thing was they had a body that would be handy in their effort to get rid of Bonner. And I emphasized that we had the advantage: We knew something of which Lacey was unaware. We knew his character and his intentions. And with the safeguards we'd put in place, we could watch his every move.

"Now," I said, "I don't want to have any knowledge when Lacey is expected to step in. I want surprise to register on my face when I first see him in the position to confirm my ignorance and make him wonder about our relationship. What's more – this is very important – stay away from The Trap."

Three weeks later, after most of the world had seen the historic walk on the moon in 1969, Donald Lacey waited in Ed Butler's office, as everyone passing by eyed him through the open door, wondering who he was. He must have felt uneasy, sitting there for all to see. He wasn't used to being a subject of curiosity. He checked his watch: 10:47 a.m. Fifteen minutes had passed. Lacey lit up a smoke and looked around, wondering what was delaying Butler.

Lacey had no idea that his situation was problematic. Butler was displeased with Lacey's apparent attempt to coerce him for his own ends. He told me he'd questioned himself and still wasn't totally convinced he should have gone along with my thinking. Butler wouldn't dare bring in anyone who would consider him a buffoon and might challenge his position in time. He'd even thought of ignoring his agreement with me – after all he had the status to do what he wanted. But to go against me would interfere with the plan to dispose of Bonner, as I'd laid it out.

While it would be somewhat awkward for him to treat Lacey professionally after having such mischievous outings together, Butler knew he had no choice; he'd been forced into that position. Just the same, he still had a score to settle, and he knew any chance he got, no matter how trivial, he would be tempted to discreetly stick a thorn in Lacey's side. So he intentionally kept Lacey waiting.

"I'm sorry for holding you up so long," Butler said, breathing heavily as he closed the door behind him. "Something pressing came up that required my immediate attention." Then, to test Lacey's candor, Butler asked if he'd kept their intent under his hat. Lacey replied that he had – that was in their best interest.

Of course, Butler knew better from his talks with me, but he didn't challenge him. Instead, he pumped Lacey with questions to give the meeting an appearance of being official. How's business? What did he see happening in the market? Was there a lot of confusion? Was he optimistic in the aftermath of the disturbances?

Lacey admitted that following King's assassination and the '67 riots things had become unraveled and business was slow. But that was not to say there was no business out there to be found. More important, he thought that with the right sales staff willing to work hard and do its homework, he could see the '70's looking very promising.

Lacey wanted to turn the subject back to raising doubts about me, and asked Butler if he saw the articles in the *Sunday Free Press* about me speaking on behalf of New Detroit.

"No, but I did receive his brochure on the new Black image of the Negro. Apart from those things you told me about him, what do you really think of him as a salesman?"

"He's different. But I can't deny he's a talented professional who believes in knowing where his market's been, where it's at, and where it's going. We've discussed business any number of times. In fact, we shared in a presentation on the Negro market, addressing a group of local agency people, sometime back," he boasted.

Butler apprised him of their corporate plans – remodeling The Tower's offices and studios, setting up retirement and health plans for the non-air staff, moving their foreign language programs to their FM frequency, and going with a twenty-four-hour Negro format (precisely the recommendation I'd made long before, though Lacey wasn't told that). Butler explained that the move would necessitate hiring two additional newsmen, a music director and three additional jocks. For the first time, all would be Negroes. Butler assumed that wouldn't be a problem for Lacey since he was now working with them. Lacey assured him it wouldn't be – he knew those people very well and could work with them.

"Well then," Butler said, "just before everything comes together I'll be in touch. Any questions?"

"Yes. How much authority will I have?"

"As much as you need to get the job done," Butler said.

"Can you give me an approximate time?"

"My guess would be very soon."

"All right," Lacey said. "I'll look forward to your call."

Later that day, Cathy called and informed me that she'd overheard I was getting a new boss. Playing dumb, I asked his name and when he was expected to come in. All Cathy could say was that he was a big man with thick black hair. But if it would help, she'd try to get more information. I thanked her and cautioned her to keep out of harm's way. I hung up, pleased. Everything was going as planned.

CHAPTER TWELVE

The elevator door closed behind me on the twentieth floor, leaving me alone with Tina, the operator. She turned to me, troubled, but didn't speak, and she wouldn't push the lever to move. Through the years, she'd dumped lots of personal problems on me, so why was she hesitating now? I waited in that closed elevator going nowhere, until finally she exploded: Her Majesty had gotten on her elevator and jumped all over her for nothing. Tina didn't understand her. One minute Her Majesty was laughing and joking, the next minute flying off the handle. "What's her problem?" Tina asked, pushing the lever down to ascend.

I'd gotten used to making excuses for Her Majesty. She was my girl; that was her way; and that's all there was to it. I soothed Tina, saying Her Majesty did the same to everyone and me. At times, she had so much on her mind she didn't know if she was coming or going. "I'm sure the next time you see her, she won't even remember, or if she does, she'll apologize."

"But it's so embarrassing," Tina said.

"I know, I know," I said gently as the elevator stopped at my floor.

When the door opened, Lacey was standing there. I feigned surprise.

"Didn't you know I was coming in today?" Lacey said.

I wanted him to think his scheme to get between me and Butler had worked, so I told him Butler hadn't communicated with me at all since I saw the two of them together at The Trap.

Now it was Lacey's turn to fake surprise. "That's strange," he said, "but now that I'm here, let's go somewhere and talk."

On our way out, I stopped to greet Karen, the new switchboard operator. As I reached for my messages, she handed me one from Lacey and said, low, "Did he tell you he's the new general sales manager?" Covering her mouth, she whispered, "I wasn't supposed to say anything until the memo on it came out." Promising her I wouldn't say a word, I rejoined Lacey, keeping a straight face.

He wanted to go get a drink, but I still had work to do, so we settled at the Flaming Embers that was filled with coffee-breakers. At a table beside a picture window that gave a view of activities on the street and in the park beyond, trails of vapor rose from the hot cups. I took a sip, while Lacey silently waited for his to cool.

At forty-four, Lacey was five years older than me. He was clean-shaven, and at his best had a rich voice ideal for a pitchman, but his eyes were dazed and bloodshot, and his physique bloated, both from too much booze. He followed the figures outside the window, as I continued to inhale the steam from my coffee, but as Lacey's silence continued, I became impatient. Finally I clinked my spoon against my cup to break his mood and get on with the show.

Having decided on his approach, Lacey began, "Though we've only spent a little time together, I've learned a lot about you from your contemporaries and from the people at the agencies. I want you to know," he said, reaching out to shake my hand, "even though this day was a long time coming, I'm thrilled to finally get this chance to work with you."

I didn't buy into his praise, and made no response, letting him wonder why. He cleared his throat and asked for one of my cigarettes. I obliged. Lacey needed to know if his gossip had succeeded in disrupting my friendship, so he exhaled and inquired innocently if there was anything wrong between me and Butler. As innocently, I replied, "None I'm aware of. Why?"

Lacey kept probing but I wanted to stay clear of it. He tried a last time, asking if I'd recently spoken to Butler about him. I dismissed it, saying that wasn't necessary, "In your case, he knew my feelings. Now let's get to the point of us being here. I have a long day ahead."

Lacey had been monitoring the station for a couple of weeks. He agreed that the jack-legged preachers should go, and thought the programming could stand more changes. I interrupted: What did his job have to do with programming? Lacey figured he could make suggestions to the program director and to Bonner. However, he didn't know how to replace the income lost after getting rid of the preachers.

I told him that's no problem – they could fill up those nighttime segments with cut-rate spots, which would be ideal for the clubs, or increase their prime time rate, or both. Lacey agreed enthusiastically then paused. He wanted to know my take on Her Majesty. "Help me out."

Nothing had changed for me since we spoke about her some years back, but I did want to hear what Lacey thought. He had no use for her. She's crude, wild and woolly. Instead of airing her grievances behind closed doors, she barked them out in the open, or worse, over the air so all could hear. "That's no way to conduct business," he said. "It's a no-win situation with her. The less I have to do with her, the better.

"However, in regards to you, I've been told that you're a long-time, key player," Lacey said as he eyed me shrewdly and put his smoke out. "I've also been told you're accessible to most of the folks up there, and that you have their unqualified respect. That puts you in the catbird seat. I'm going to need your thinking and cooperation to do my job. Can I depend on it?"

The point of the meeting had finally come down. I looked away, knowing that question would sooner or later pop up. I'd been around the block with his predecessors, and obliged each one on cue with my advice when they were in need, but never received any credit. Worse, they ignored me when business was running smoothly. I'd vowed never again to be used as a crutch or even as a sounding board for anyone in charge. Still, I'd allow Lacey just enough to get a bead on how he'd act towards me. I took another sip of coffee, prolonging his wait for my response before I said, "That goes without saying, if you're fair in your dealings."

"You can count on that," Lacey said.

Penelope, Her Majesty's secretary, was waiting impatiently on the elevator when I returned. She looked glum, but managed a big smile as I came toward her and asked what was wrong. She sighed heavily – it hadn't been a good morning. They were in the process of moving their office down to the eighteenth floor.

"Why the move?"

Penelope told me that Lacey was taking over Her Majesty's office and that she hit the ceiling and went on the wild, biting off everybody's head. But thanks to God, she's calmed down a little because Mitch, Her Majesty's manager, got the contract to manage the building for the new owner, and he arranged a suite of offices they would share.

I suspected it was best that she move off the floor, putting plenty of space between her and Lacey. Even so, I recognized that this part of my plan was moving much faster than I'd anticipated.

A little over a week later, Karl Kruger burst angrily into Bonner's office and slammed the door behind him. He said Lacey had just told him to cancel his churches or Lacey would do it.

"What's his problem? Is he out of his fucking skull! Can he do that?" Karl shouted loud enough for some of the staff to hear.

Bonner dropped his head, and then answered, "I suppose so. He's the general sales manager now."

Karl wanted to know if Bonner was part of it, and if not, couldn't he block Lacey before it was too late?

As quiet as it was kept, Bonner had deferred taking the preachers off the air some time ago simply because he couldn't bring himself to pull it off, knowing Karl had several kids and very little on the books beside the churches. So when Lacey arrived and approached Bonner about it, he immediately saw a way to keep his hands pure by making Lacey the scapegoat. He knew he could no longer cover Karl's tracks. And he understood that Butler not only knew about this change – he agreed to it. So he suggested Karl get in touch with Butler. "Speak about the money," Bonner advised. Then he dialed Butler's extension and handed the phone to Karl.

Karl appealed to Butler, arguing they'd be throwing a lot of money away for nothing. And look at the shape it would leave him in. Couldn't he put a stop to it?

Butler said Lacey already assured him he could make up the loss. In any case, Mr. Beck gave Lacey permission, not him. Butler said there was nothing he could do, though Karl could try convincing Lacey to keep the preachers, himself.

"Dammit!" Karl exclaimed as he hung up. "For sixteen years I've been working my ass off. Then here comes this Donald Lacey throwing out all my hard work in a matter of days, leaving me nothing! You said you couldn't do anything. Ed says he can't do anything. Where does the buck stop? I'm left out on a limb. Christ, what kind of job security do we have around this damn place? Sixteen years down the tube because that son of a bitch doesn't like my churches. Well, I'm not going to take this crap. I'm not canceling anything!"

At the same time, I was talking to Lacey in his office. He didn't care that Karl was probably teed off with him. His orders were clear. Now I'd have to follow through and get my clubs to buy up the time. If I figured right, Karl would leave. Lacey said he would have to get someone to replace him, though, and that might present a problem because he had no accounts to give him to get started.

"This is where I need your help when the time comes," Lacey said with a pretense of ruefulness. "I'll need at least three agencies from you, one big and two not so big, but workable. And I need you to start thinking about your choices. Any questions?"

Silence fell. The suddenness of Lacey's request threw me. My reservations notwithstanding, I tried to reason objectively. I held most of the working accounts. However, I'd worked long hours for most, sometimes even into the late evening and morning hours to service my clubs. I earned everything I had. Why should I give up any? On the other hand, Karl's annoying presence and his irritating jack-legged preachers would finally hit the dust. While those would be blessings, still, Lacey's request... well, it was a bit too much.

I didn't have a question; I had a statement. I told Lacey I was uncomfortable with his request. I didn't happen on this job – I planned for it, even though, at first, it offered very little. I was blind when starting in sales, and received not a blessed thing but a desk and a list of retailers copied right out of the phone directory. Still, I'd worked hard from scratch for what I'd gotten.

"What's more," I said, "I was the only one back then daring enough to pioneer and crack open the agencies. My accounts mean more to me than the mere loss of revenue. An earned relationship of trust, built over the years is in jeopardy as well. You should already know that your request is a no-no to me. As you once told me, nobody gave you anything; you had to work for everything you got. Well, I'm telling you the same goes in my case."

"I know your feelings, believe me," Lacey said. "It hurts for me to ask. We have so much in common."

"The only thing we have in common is that we work at the same place."

"No, we have more than that. We're both tough. We're both aggressive and we're not afraid to go after what we want. We're both... Anyway," he gestured dismissively, "I have no choice. You're the only one who has anything that amounts to something. I won't ask this again—just this time. You have my word."

I had a knack for observing Lacey beneath his animated demeanor and his rich, commanding voice. I felt almost like I could pierce into his soul where his words were garbled and fuzzy. They smacked of hollow lies teetering upon the limits I had set for him. And while my gut feelings of distrust for him were steadily rising, I knew that time was still my ally, and in time, Lacey's true self would be unveiled by his actions. If my thinking proved correct, that would be the day Lacey would be vanquished.

In 1969, 250,000 war protesters holding peace signs fanned out from the capitol in Washington, D.C., "Midnight Cowboy" hustled the streets of New York, and "Easy Rider" captured a generation's yearning to be free of the establishment.

Meanwhile, at The Tower, events were moving swiftly. Karl Kruger had been on a merry-go-round trying to sell a market he knew little about. Now his jack-legged preachers were shot to the curb, and his two main supporters abandoned him, leaving him no longer able to defend his position. There was no place for him to go but out.

Soon afterward, Henry Kolinsky took his foreign language accounts off FM and left, as well, to take over sales at another foreign language station. Once Henry was gone, that left three salesmen, including me. Lacey wanted one more, and he called me to his office.

Lacey was on the phone when I entered, and continued his conversation while I waited. Minutes passed as I sat there, observing Lacey's pompous, cavalier posturing, interspersed with self-congratulatory glances in my direction. Lacey was in his glory, but I had no time for that. I got up to leave. Immediately Lacey hung up and stood.

He told me his objectives were coming loose at the seams but he knew he could mend things with a little more help from me. "I'll come right to the point," he said without wavering, "I need another salesman to build the staff to where I want it so I can make my projections for this year."

I noticed an all too familiar twitch in Lacey's jaw, a quirk that came out whenever he was about to ask something far-fetched. And though I saw a train bearing down on me, I couldn't believe it. Lacey wouldn't dare! There's no way Lacey could think I was that gullible!

"...I know you won't like my request. Still, I must ask you to give up a few more accounts."

Though I had a strong inkling of this coming, it was still unbelievable that Lacey's word was so fragile that he'd have the audacity to ask that of me again. I considered it an outrageous disregard of my rights and intelligence. No way would I allow Lacey to make his mark by riding my back. And what about Henry's working accounts? Wasn't Lacey going to give them up, or were they going to be kept as house accounts? I refused to respond. It was all I could do to keep my cool intact.

After getting no rise from me, Lacey prodded, "You must understand..."

"Understand what?" I shot back. "Understand that you neglected to say that your plan to build a sales staff relied on using my agencies as the stimulus? What's more, you took the accounts I gave you, and instead of bringing in a Black man who understood the market, you hired your white friend who knew nothing – and then you had the nerve to ask me to teach him. What a laugh! You've tried my patience, man. Your character is parasitic, destructive, always asking for something and never giving. You're trying to move too damn fast to make an impression, and you're failing. You must think you're talking to a fool or a Stepin Fetchit, or one of those Amos'n'Andy types you were raised up on. If that's what you think, you're dead wrong, muh man!"

Lacey back-pedaled fast. "That's not it. I definitely know you're not a fool. Why would you accuse me of that? You really know how to push my button, don't you?"

I said nothing.

It didn't matter. Lacey believed he had risen above me in Butler's eyes, and had the power to do anything he wanted. He warned me, "I'll get the accounts one way or another, but I'd rather we negotiate. Work with me. Can't we make a deal? Don't worry—I'll take care of you. When things get going I'm thinking about making you my assistant."

"Oh, goody, goody gum drops. That's mighty white of you, sir. If that's your idea of conciliation, I'm not buying. Climb down off your mercy seat, man!" And I walked out sharply, leaving Lacey wide-eyed and flustered.

To make sure Lacey wouldn't forget my position, I spelled it out in a long letter that covered not only my tenure of fourteen years but also what I was about as a Black man, and what I knew was the attitude of ownership. The letter left nothing, absolutely nothing, between the lines. More than a month passed before Lacey made an appointment to discuss it.

We met at the Detroit Hilton for early lunch at 11:30, and avoided the issues with trivial conversation in the beginning. It wasn't until the dishes were cleared that we faced each other, each of us defensive, dancing on eggshells so no vulnerabilities were exposed, neither of us giving an inch. At first Lacey attempted to explain why it was right for him to request my accounts. That brought nothing from me but silence as I fixed my eyes on his, separating the half-truths from the downright lies.

As time passed and drinks continued, our tongues lost their stiffness and the civility of our dialogue became overwhelmed with clenched teeth retorts. Each time I tripped Lacey in a lie, he blamed it on the booze. Soon we were pitted in battle like two gamecocks oblivious of our surroundings. I could see that the drinks had gotten to Lacey. With his drinking reputation he was surprised to see me hang tough round for round. Little did he know that I'd already figured he was the type to try to get me drunk and use any slip to his advantage. So, after the third round, each time Lacey took his weak bladder off to "pay a water bill," I emptied my martini into my water glass and asked the waitress to replace the water.

So my rhythm was with me, my reflexes sharp, and I was able to pursue my advantage. Like a boxer, I countered Lacey's moves instinctively, avoiding his efforts to clinch or slip punches, attacking any minor flaw to back him into a corner. My memory compared to Lacey's was impeccable. Over time, Lacey's peremptory tone and physical animation vanished, as his speech became thick. Unless he admitted he had been wrong, there was nothing fitting for Lacey to say or do, because every consonant and every vowel of my carefully crafted letter had flayed him bare of his false pretenses.

Lacey's ego was badly bruised. I could see the veins in his neck. As the old saying goes, I had his water on and it was boiling when

Lacey terminated the luncheon abruptly by pounding the table top with his fist and rising to proclaim, "I'm the general sales manger, and I'll do as I damn please! Quit if you don't like it!"

I had thought I was a good judge of character, but what I'd believed about Lacey in the very beginning might not be the man he was turning out to be. Lacey's foibles had come to light, and I decided at this moment to suppress my emotions, to be cool, careful not to be a fool by volleying back in anger. If I could leave Lacey to grapple with his preposterous remark about me quitting, then my own lack of action should surely pop Lacey's veins.

I was not about to surrender my manhood or any more of my accounts. I'd sit tight, undaunted, measuring the infuriation swelling Lacey's six-foot-four inch frame that dwarfed the two-seat table. I lit up a smoke, whiffed a smoke-ring across the table, and then turned away, ignoring Lacey completely, while I slowly glanced about the room, finding it deserted but for three patrons at the bar. I checked my watch and placed it to my ear. Its ticking punctuated this unbelievable situation. I became amused not only at the time spent with this whole ordeal, but also with Lacey's bungling, imperious attitude, which told me I had prevailed. I knew how to handle Lacey now, and a piquant smile passed my lips.

Lacey's mouth dropped, gaping in uncertainty. I imagined him as a tire whose air was slowly leaking, as I stared back at him in blank dismay. Without question, Lacey's distress with me was clearly visible before he turned away and staggered off, passing the big clock on the wall that showed twelve midnight.

I needed to slow the events down; the time was not yet right. But it was time to take advantage of an invitation to visit Her Majesty and Mitch in their new environment to bring them up to speed. She was one of the last missing links that would just about solidify my *thang*.

"You like?" Her Majesty asked, taking my hand, as I admired the artful décor. I hollered to Penelope who was in the conference room, but Her Majesty pulled me to see Mitch who was waiting in his office.

Mitch, an ex-third-string New York Giant quarterback who never got his chance to lead on the field of play, posed a handsome figure by anyone's standard – tall, well built, with a rich, black, curly afro. His neatly trimmed goatee and his yellow, suntanned complexion led many to see him as anything but Black. I'd met him some years back when he was pushing records, long before becoming Her Majesty's manager, and I'd taken to him like butter to toast. Mitch was fun, though at times his childlike frankness could be ferociously foul.

He was standing over his big mahogany desk, playing out the entrepreneurial role he had envisioned for years. I noticed he looked snappy, with a red rose tucked into the lapel of his gray, sharkskin, three-piece *vine*. Now his hair was fashioned to drop to his neckline, and that gave a maturity to his thirty-six years. As I entered, he was lighting up a long, thin stogie, a style he'd acquired to enhance his new status.

"Hey, Mr. Big Time, you looking pretty cool. But be careful how ya light dat thing, y'undastan? Don't singe your goatee or choke yo'se'f to death," I jested.

"No way, muh man. I can handle it. I've cultivated a taste for these muthas. How in the hell are you," he beamed, holding out a stogie. "Here, try one of these muthas, it'll rattle your balls and make your asshole sing."

"No thanks, baby, I giggled. "Anything that messes with my nature in that manner, I don't need."

As we laughed, Her Majesty interjected, "He don't have much time, Mitch. Y'all quit shuckin' and jivin' and get on with the business we're here for."

After getting their commitment to keep the meeting in strictest confidence, I proceeded. I wanted to know Mitch's feelings. As far as Mitch was concerned, "Lacey couldn't stand niggahs challenging him."

I reacted seriously, "What niggahs? I don't believe I've seen any. You ought to drop that word like a hot piece of coal, muh man. It strains the Black conception and buys into some people's stereotypical views."

"Hey, it's just a figure of speech, man. Don't get rattled. You know damn well I wasn't using it the way some folks do – it don't mean a damn thing to me in turns of us folks. You gotta know that. Still, if I've offended you, I'm sorry. ...Anyway, getting back to Lacey, he's an abrasive, redneck racist who needs to get his fucking ass kicked in order to relate to what's happening. How do you see him?"

I saw Lacey differently. I didn't believe he was a racist. I'd known racists and knew their psyche – racism was all they knew. Their egos needed it to feed upon because it gave them an illusion of superiority over those to whom their hatred was aimed. They were hopelessly sick, and I had no prescription for them.

I said, "Lacey doesn't fit that type. He's just a tyrannical creature who sees everyone at The Tower and at The Buhl as inferior to his intelligence, all under his thumb to be manipulated by the enchantment of his salesmanship. He's a man who is as big as his insatiable appetite for power, a man not to be trusted. A disingenuous anathema..."

"A what?" Her Majesty howled.

"An anathema," I chuckled, "a person who is disliked or loathed."

"You got that right, my dear boy. My goodness gracious, don't tell me you've finally seen him in the full light. What did I tell you? Lord have mercy!" she exclaimed in delight. Then she added, "What about Butler?"

I was reluctant to reveal my relationship with Butler at this time – it wouldn't have served any purpose. Besides, Butler was my ace in the hole to hold and uncover in my own time. So I said, "I've had very little contact with Butler, so I can't say." Still, I wanted to know if Bonner was still teaching Ted the rudiments of management. After being assured he was, I let them in on my objectives at the station, wisely omitting my plan for Bonner. Though both were amazed by my long-term strategy, they readily gave their approval. I cautioned them to be cool until the time was right.

Lacey's freewheeling approach soon reached beyond sales. He

shuffled the jocks' airtime around, usurping the authority of Barry Atwater, the program director, and raising the ire of the air-staff. Her Majesty relayed the complaints to Bonner. Because Lacey had come in through Butler, Bonner relayed the charges to him. Butler then called me and got confirmation. Knowing Butler's attitude toward Lacey, I told him not to panic but to call Lacey to his office, listen to his lies, then dismiss him. I also reminded him of the purpose for which Lacey was hired and assured Butler that after our objective was accomplished, I'd take Lacey on.

In Butler's office, Lacey contended there was no problem. Butler informed him what Bonner had told him about Lacey creating a morale problem for the jocks. If that was true, sooner or later it was going to get back to Mr. Beck. "Before that happens, I have to know what's going on over there," Butler insisted.

Lacey had to defend himself, arguing he was putting together a better programming schedule to generate better numbers in drive time. So he switched Moonman to morning drive because he was more up-beat, and put Motormouth in afternoon drive. He also switched Barry to nighttime. Lacey implored Butler not to get alarmed over Bonner's negative apprehensions – he knew what he was doing, and in time, it would all work out fine. His only problem now was doing away with Her Majesty's show in favor of a more consistent music format. But, Lacey complained, every time he approached Bonner about it, he turned a deaf ear.

Lacey said, "You just don't have a religious-type service in the middle of a rhythm'n'blues format. That's crazy! You got to get behind me, Ed."

"How can I?" Butler led him on.

"Number one, get Bonner off my back so I can let Her Majesty go." For his second wish, Lacey asked Butler to make me give up three of my accounts so he could hire another salesman.

Butler answered, "I might be able to help you out on number one, but I'm helpless on the second. There's nothing in his contract that says he must give up accounts he's put on the books. In fact, I was really surprised to find out he'd already given some up for that other salesman you hired."

I always knew Lacey had a begrudging respect for me, but since our lunch I also realized that the total control Lacey demanded would be impossible as long as I worked at The Tower. It was a long shot at best, but Lacey figured it wouldn't do any harm to ask Butler what he really wanted.

"Then suppose I got rid of him," Lacey said, "and hired two or three more good salesmen in his place. Would I have your support?"

"He's by far our best salesman," Butler responded. "Even you told me how impressed you were with him. Why would you want to do that?"

Lacey knew he would have to come up with a story that would sound believable. He admitted he was impressed with me before he got to work with me closely. But after knowing me, he said he found me to be a troublemaker who showed no respect for him. Lacey mentioned a contest he wanted to put on, which I believed was offensive to my market, so I refused to be a part of it.

Lacey complained, "Every chance he gets, he plays hardball and dumps on me. He even stormed out on me a couple of times, not to mention that he considers Muhammad Ali a hero because he wouldn't step forward and fight for our cause in Vietnam. Imagine that! That alone is proof enough that he's a Black militant. All he ever talks about are the Blacks. Except for him, I don't know any Blacks. I only know Negroes. I'm sick of it!"

Butler had listened, but all the while he saw Lacey as a threat. It had taken all Butler could muster to keep from ordering him out of his office, reminding himself he had promised to play along.

Finally, Butler said, "I'm not particularly keen on that Black type of thinking, but you're asking the impossible. There's nothing I can do about him. Even if I could, there's no guarantee the salesmen replacing him would be as productive." And Butler reminded Lacey that Mr. Beck was no fool. He was a businessman. The business I brought in not only paid my own way but helped pay some of the staff's salaries as well. "He's making Mr. Beck money," Butler stated. "That's the bottom line to him. He would see through your scheme right away."

Butler reminded Lacey that he was the one responsible for him being there, and if he fired me, that would leave Butler in jeopardy as well. And that's a slippery slope he dare not step on. However, Butler said he could do something about Bonner and would meet with him tomorrow. Meanwhile, "Do whatever you can to get your respect," but he'd better leave me alone.

The minute Lacey left, Butler phoned and brought me up to date. He agreed with me that it was time to move ahead with our plan.

CHAPTER THIRTEEN

The next day, though the skies were gloomy, Bonner hummed a happy tune as he walked briskly along Woodward Avenue towards The Buhl. He hardly noticed the crowds or the traffic, searching his mind why Butler had said, "it's very important" for Bonner to be there first thing in the morning. It had to be the vice presidency, he had finally concluded. It was a long time in coming, but better late than never. Now he would sit on the board, and with a status equal to Butler's, he would no longer have to take his insults or barbs. And he'd finally be able to put Lacey in his place, show him whose boss, and get The Tower back under his helm. He smiled to himself.

His steps quickened as he left the elevator. He'd never felt this good, ever, coming to see Butler. What had seemed a dreary walk in the past was different this morning as he whisked through the long corridor smiling at everyone along the way.

Removing his hat, he greeted Dorothy, the receptionist, "Mr. Butler is expecting me. Is he in his office?"

He stepped out for a minute, she said. Butler had told her to have Bonner wait. He headed for Butler's office but she stopped him, "No sir, not in his office—over there, please."

Bonner rested his coat and took one of the seats along the wall. As he sat there, he wondered why Butler was not on time and why he'd been placed here, like a nobody, and not in Butler's office. Butler had said first thing in the morning. Something unexpected probably came up. Oh well, he shouldn't be long.

Ten minutes passed, then fifteen. Bonner was beginning to steam inside, wondering if the little rat was up to his old tricks. He asked Dorothy if she had any idea where he went. All she knew was that Butler had gone to breakfast. She didn't like lying, but Butler had instructed her specifically where to seat Bonner and what to say. She confided to me later that it seemed as if lying was most of what she did on Butler's behalf – the little stinker.

Finally the phone rang, and she was able to tell Bonner, "That was him. He's on his way."

Butler was in no hurry, dillydallying along, looking in store windows. He knew Bonner hated to wait on anyone, especially him. All along, Butler's scheme was to unbalance him a bit and make him more vulnerable to his sting. When he came through The Buhl's entrance and saw Bonner all red-faced, he knew the initial part of his plan was working. No greetings were exchanged.

"I don't need to tell you how time in this business gets messed around. Why are you sitting there instead of my office? That's no place for the general manager of The Tower," he said, turning aside to give Dorothy a wink.

"C'mon, let's get started," Butler, continued as he entered his office. "I imagine you want to get back to your work. Close the door behind you..."

"Is Mr. Beck joining us?"

"No, he won't be along."

Bonner sat and tried to relax. He thought it odd that on such an occasion Mr. Beck wouldn't be present. But then, Mr. Beck has many involvements, so why trouble him unnecessarily.

Butler began that he'd spoken to Lacey about his concerns, and they sounded reasonable, unless there was more to it than he'd been told. Was there?

Bonner complained the problem wasn't what Lacey did but how he went about it. You don't suddenly change a jock's time-slot without giving him ample notice to adjust. And you don't do that in secrecy, disregarding the program director. Bonner said that even he knew nothing about it until all hell broke out. At the very least, Lacey should have talked it over so Bonner could have advised him how to do it right.

Butler also asked about Her majesty, agreeing with Lacey that they should give her the boot. But Bonner countered that she was one of the station's most important draws. He knew her show didn't fit their format, but their audience didn't seem to care. He reminded Butler that some of that time used to be given away as bonus spots until she came, and now it's not only filled up, but also beating out drive time at a higher premium rate. Her audience loved her, and Bonner believed if they dropped her show, the community would rebel against the station.

"I can't bring myself to believe that," Butler said.

"That's because you're sitting on your butt in this ivory tower. You're an accountant, Ed. You have no idea what's going on out there. You allowed a young whipper-snapper to come in, do as he pleased, disrupt the place, and cause unrest at the station. You should be ashamed of yourself. That's where your ignorance of this business shows," Bonner railed, surprising Butler as well as himself.

Butler sat as tall as gravity would allow and blustered, "That may be true, but around here and over there, I'm still the one whose decisions are final, except for Mr. Beck. So if you want to get along, you better stay on my good side or you'll be looking for another employer."

Hurt, and realizing the meeting wasn't what he had thought, Bonner had no reason not to challenge Butler. Like teenage boys, they lashed out at one another, wavering on the brink of a bare-knuckle brawl that startled the staff nearby that stopped working to watch. When the dust settled, Bonner abruptly got up to leave.

"Think what you want," Bonner said, "but you didn't hire me, and you can't fire me, and I'm not about to listen to any more of your crap."

"Maybe I can't, but Mr. Beck sure can. You know the rules about lying. If you break the rules, you're off the payroll."

"What the hell are you talking about?" Bonner challenged.

"Didn't you once tell him you'd worked on Mr. Lee's account?"

"That was long ago. I don't remember."

"Well, I do. And I know you didn't work on it."

"You can't prove that!" Bonner fought back.

"Oh, but I can. You better sit back down before you fall on your face."

Butler had waited patiently over the years for the chance to go for Bonner's jugular. The time was now. Anxiously, he dialed his phone and switched on his speaker. At the other end, I'd been waiting on this call. As planned, Butler asked me to think back to the time I'd gotten the expansive contract from Mr. Lee, and describe what part Bonner played in getting it.

"None," I said, "except for adding the bonus spots later."

"Is that the absolute truth? Are you sure?" Butler probed.

"Certainly – why would I lie? Why are you asking?"

"Oh, no reason—I was just thinking back about it, and I thought Bonner might have played some part. If not, thank you."

Butler hung up, gloating over Bonner's predicament, "Is that enough proof, or should I call Lee to get more verification?"

Bonner was too stunned to say anything. While he knew Butler was a sneak freak, he would never have imagined he'd go that far back in time to put him under the gun. Bonner sank back into his seat, struggling to reset himself. Finally, with resentment swelling his eyes, he stared at his old nemesis, sighed heavily, and then said, "Tell me what you want?"

"I'm in a generous mood today," Butler proclaimed with self-importance. "I tell you what: you have two choices. Either I expose your lie to Mr. Beck, which would get you fired with no benefits. Or, at your age, you can retire at the end of the year and save your pension. How are those choices?" he smiled triumphantly.

His dream shot, weary and disheveled, Bonner hit the door. The once-proud captain, who had played his role so well by concealing his weakness, found himself in a position similar to all the others he'd vanquished. It was a sort of poetic justice, but to Bonner it was heart wrenching. He'd been turned inside out and was blindly groping his way along the now long, dreary corridor. Through the streets he had come, he returned. Thwarted in his attempt to leave The Tower in his own time, he never suspected the end could come about this way. "The little shrimp," he muttered. "If only I could be sure I wouldn't have to suffer the consequences, I'd choke the living crap out of Butler."

At The Tower, Bonner didn't bother picking up his messages and headed straight for his office. Behind his closed door, he slumped down in his seat, dejected, and mulled over what had just transpired. Seething, his eyes welling with tears, he envisioned Lacey's satisfaction when he'd get the word. Then his thoughts veered back to Butler, "that rotten, little shit," he mumbled under his breath.

Reluctantly, he got his messages from the switchboard and absently returned some calls, stewing in his anger. Vaguely, he could hear Her Majesty's broadcast through the intercom; he hit the switchboard extension again and left word to have her come to him immediately after her show. Then he turned up the volume on the intercom. She seemed to be talking directly to him.

"...In times of sorrow, let not the negativity of some folks creep into your life to humble you and bring you down more. Sincerely ask God to give you strength and His guidance. Then straighten your back, lift your head, and walk tall, knowing your sorrow will soon be something in the past..."

As Bonner listened, feeling a measure of relief, he checked his watch against the big clock on the wall. Two o'clock was slow in coming.

"...I'm telling you what I know from experience. God knew that I, as a young divorcee with three small girls to raise and no job didn't know what to do. All He wanted me to do was ask Him for His help and guidance. That I did through His son Jesus, and you know what? I haven't looked back since..."

Bonner listened on and on while gazing up towards the ceiling. As she closed down her show, he took out his handkerchief and dabbed at his eyes. He tightened his tie, straightened in his seat, and waited stiffly.

"It's unlocked, come in," Bonner called out,

Her Majesty's full robe flowed to her ankles and left the contours of her shapely forty-something full figure to the imagination. She sat before him gracefully.

"What's going on, Mr. Bonner? You look stressed out," she said, regarding him closely as she waited for him to compose himself enough to answer.

Bonner smoothed over the imaginary wrinkles in his desk pad. He had long since abandoned his notions of having her favors. She was now his confidante, the only consoling listener with whom he could bear his soul, receive her spiritual inspiration and then leave thinking the world of him. But this day, he wasn't in the mood to sing any sad songs, only wanted to take care of the work on his desk and take off. But he knew he'd have to tell her of his and her bleak fate.

"That was an enlightening message you gave today," he finally said in a frail voice. "It was truly timely for me. You just can't imagine what my day has been like. I can hardly believe it myself." He paused, shaking his head, and made him say what he must, "I have some disappointing news to tell you. But you must promise not to breathe a word of it just yet. Promise?"

She promised, but he couldn't find the courage to tell her the whole truth that he was getting shot to the curb by a man he'd always sworn was a pip-squeak. So he said he was being forced into retirement because of his age.

"Who's going to be your replacement? Don't tell me Donald Lacey, please. That's all I need to hear to start me screaming."

He nodded – probably it was true. Despite what everyone believed, he didn't have any voice in bringing Lacey to the station. Lacey was Ed Butler's golden haired boy. If the choice had been his, he actually would have gone for me, despite my feelings about him. His eyes watered as he confessed he'd made some mistakes and a few were in his dealings with me. "Now, I guess, I must suffer the consequences."

"We all make mistakes, Mr. Bonner," she said with sympathy. Then she asked why Mr. Beck hadn't chosen me, considering my track record.

"It's too embarrassing," Bonner muttered.

Her Majesty encouraged him; "I thought we had the kind of friendship where we could talk about anything. Has that changed?"

"Of course not—you should know that would never happen. You've brought so much sunshine into my life here. If you hadn't come along at the time you did, I don't know what I would've done. Probably I would've been long gone."

Bonner had never felt this uneasy in her company, struggling to find the words for something he didn't want to say. But, with all that had happened that day, he saw nothing good coming about if he didn't tell her the truth.

He said that Mr. Beck was very pleased with my work as a salesman. However, he didn't think Jews or Negroes should be put in leadership positions. "Believe me, I'm ashamed to tell you, but that's the real reason he didn't get the sales manager position."

"Then he was right all along," Her Majesty mused, thinking back on what I'd told her. "I didn't want to believe him because the reason sounded so stupid. I thought it might've been a personal thing between you two," she said.

Bonner defended himself that not only did he think the reason was stupid, but it also made people think he was a racist. "You know I'm not," he pleaded for her to assure him. Bonner went on to blame all the racist decisions on Mr. Beck who then subjugated him to carry them out under the guise of company policies, even though that did Mr. Beck more harm than good.

But that wasn't the end of the difficult things he had to say that day. "Finally," he went on, dropping his voice, "I saved the worst news for last." His hand shook and his voice quavered as he struggled for the right words to explain her fate. He just didn't know how to be diplomatic about it. All he knew was how sorry he was at that moment.

"Lacey is determined to drop your show," he said. "I wish I could come up with something that would prevent it, but I can't. I'm a little too old now to start fighting the system. The only comfort I can give, with a bit of certainty, is that it's unlikely to happen until the first of the year when I'm gone."

That didn't give Her Majesty very much time. It was a personal thing between Lacey and herself; a vendetta Lacey held against her for the many times she had disregarded his presence during their days at WDDD. Now that her show was in real jeopardy, quick moves were needed.

"What about Ted? Are you still working with him?" she scrambled for reassurance that what she'd told me was correct – that someone was learning the rudiments of management. When Bonner confirmed that, she mentioned that she and I had been thinking about "something." And without letting him in on the plan, she said, "When it comes together I'll be back to get your support and blessing."

"Anything, anything you want, I'll do. You know," he said, reaching out to her, looking into her eyes, "you're a very strong woman. You took the news far better than me, and much better than I'd imagined."

She smiled. But as she left, her thoughts turned back to her conversation with me. What did I mean: "When the time is right?"

CHAPTER FOURTEEN

Despite his impasse with me, Lacey zealously continued to throw around his two hundred and fifty-four pounds. He was on the fringe of lunacy but nothing would deter him from his hot pursuit of Bonner's chair. He put the word out on Bonner's coming retirement and instigated rumors about doing away with Her Majesty and a few others. Soon the gossip found legs of its own, invading every door and every ear, creating a bleak climate of suspicion that fermented the seeds of conflict. That atmosphere became the backdrop for all that was to come.

Even though the rumors about Her Majesty put her future and reputation perilously at risk, she was a formidable opponent. With a stinging wrath that could be dangerously venomous, she vowed to protect her shows by any means necessary. Time was getting near. And it was time for Her Majesty, Mitch (her manager) and me to find some means of repelling and neutralizing Lacey before he took complete control.

We concocted a plan to have Her Majesty persuade Bonner to draw up an agreement making Lacey and Ted Dawson responsible for matters concerning the air staff, mandating that the two had to work in concert. The master key was that neither Lacey nor Ted would have the authority to hire, fire, or demote without an accord.

The scheme we had in mind was a crapshoot containing several "ifs," all of which needed to be dispatched if it was going to work. But that didn't make much difference to the three of us. More important was the character of some who would be caught up in the net; that would make the whole intriguing plot feasible. The time had come to test the waters. And, as far as Her Majesty was concerned, she was taking her chances with a pair of loaded dice.

In Bonner's office, she told him the plot and explained its ramifications. He was pleased to no end and complied all too eagerly. And why not? She was still his confidante, and he was still the general manager, even if Lacey didn't treat him that way.

So after Her Majesty got all the jocks to sign the agreement, Lacey didn't have much choice but to sign as well, even though Ted was named Assistant General Manager to Bonner. Now, what did that really mean? It would seem not to have any legitimacy since The Buhl was not a party to it. That was the beauty of the ruse. We wanted Lacey to think the agreement was meaningless.

While all this was brewing at the station in 1969, the revolution took on a different complexion in Black communities compared to the white side of town. Enraged by the Vietnam War, white young people were burning their draft cards and crying "Hell no! We won't go!" Many left for Canada or joined communes, and thousands survived three great rainstorms and tons of mud declaring their freedom from the "establishment" at Woodstock. For four days they danced in rapture with Richie Havens, Joan Baez, Joe Cocker, Santana, Crosby, Stills and Nash, Sly Stone, Janis Joplin, Jimi Hendrix, and many other voices of their generation. Their cry was "Make love, not war."

Elsewhere, the Chicago Seven were being tried for their part in the antiwar protests during the '68 Democratic National Convention. And women were burning their bras to symbolize their liberation, as the Women's Movement pressed for equal pay for equal work.

In the Black communities, it was all about pride and self-determination, pulling further apart from the rest of American society. While Nina Simone's "Young, Gifted and Black" expressed the community's hope, James Weldon Johnson's "Lift Every Voice and Sing" emerged to reclaim its status as the Black National Anthem. Black folks and Negroes stood when it was played, whereas many Blacks remained seated when they heard "The Star Spangled Banner."

On the East and West sides of Detroit, giant murals of Black heroes filled "Walls of Black Pride." A group of factory workers forged the League of Revolutionary Black Workers. They, along with white activist brothers, attacked the white-dominated UAW (the United Auto Workers union) for what they called "collaborationist and racist policies."

Meanwhile, the Black community heaped honors on Judge George Crockett, Jr. for dispensing justice never before experienced by people in the community, when he presided over a case involving the Republic of New Africa and the Detroit police. In the "New Bethel Church Incident," as it came to be called, white police attacked members of the Republic of New Africa, who fought back, and this time, white police were killed or injured instead of Blacks. Like so much media coverage through the decades, the white press reported the "New Bethel Incident" in a way at best confusing and at worst rampant with racial hysteria. But now the Black community knew better than to believe what they read.

The Guardians, a national Black police officers association, which had formed to right the injustices done to its members and the community, became more visible. Richard Austin, the first Black candidate for mayor, lost by only 6,194 votes. The first Miss Black Michigan pageant was presented in the community; and the first soul commercial, produced by Blacks for a national advertiser (Kool cigarettes), hit the airwaves.

Black sisters threw away their wig-hats and adorned their heads with beautiful Afros, dreadlocks or cornrows. Dashikis and other African garb, worn proudly, were no longer inconspicuous, and along with African fashions, Swahili words infused the language on the streets. And advocates of teaching Black History in the public schools were finally being heard.

At a time when the people who were actually in power feared shouts of "All Power to the People", communication, even socializing, strangely improved between the races. White folks, in general, were introduced to Black folks' soul – their music, dance, food, their way of talkin' and walkin', and their innovative athleticism on the field and courts of sports.

Except for those Negroes who held out rigid hands, the handshake of self-determination became a graphic symbol of unity that crossed more white and Black hands than people in power recognized. And the word on the street was "Everythang's everythang."

In 1970, at the dawn of Aquarius, Diana Ross left the Supremes and boldly set out on her solo career; and Muhammad Ali returned to the ring, beating the white boxer, Jerry Quarry.

Now the Black community came of age politically. It pooled its voting strength with others of good will to gain three City Councilmen, nine Judges, a Wayne County Sheriff, three County Supervisors, three State Senators, twelve State Representatives; and Richard Austin, the Black mayoral candidate who had lost the last mayoral election, was elected Secretary of State. The revolution of the mind was at work. And many Negroes who had played no part in the Struggle jumped on the bandwagon and became "Blacker than thou."

From the confluence of all these experiences, and many more, a spiritual rebirth swept the community. The Black market had finally found its elusive Black bond that gave it a sense of empowerment and an urgency to Struggle on and support its own candidates who would be responsive to its needs and rights. It was a time to embrace their Blackness, and dispense the vile lies and fairy tales of oppression, to shed old attitudes and customs, and reach out to the new. The Black Giant had awakened! A deep sense of optimism floated in the air.

Thus the centerpiece needed to gain my target was now in place. My wait would soon be over.

At Her Majesty's conference table, the three of us—Her Majesty,

Mitch and I—discussed our next move. To offset the rumors, Her Majesty and Mitch wanted to get into the final step now, but I saw it differently. While I believed that the time was right, and timing was everything, the tealeaves spoke of a different slant. It seemed to me that if we allowed Lacey a little time to violate the agreement and fall for the *okie doke* (if we let him walk into our trap), we'd then have a legal reason to come down on him. After some discussion, both agreed with me.

I moved on with other parts of the secret plan and asked if Mitch had talked with Mr. Kupelian, the new owner of the building about our *thang*. Mitch had, and boasted there were several vacant floors in the building, which he'd gotten permission to use to suit his purpose. "That's not all," Mitch went on, "he's giving us free access to his attorney. Do we have a good *thang* or not? You can't beat that with a stick, right?"

I could hardly wait to get to Kasuku to bring him up to speed. At his den, he and I had an exhaustive examination of the current status at The Tower and what was about to happen. Kasuku wanted to know how many were involved and if their heads were on straight. I could only assure him that some who were black in color had claimed they were also Black in mind, even though I'd seen them act and think mostly like Oreos (black on the outside, white on the inside). But I said that even if some were Oreos, "We'll still have a good *thang* going. We can keep them harnessed. Plus, you'll have a chance to see and quiz them."

"Okay, little bruh. If you can convince me that your people are ready, me and my warriors will be only too happy to hook up."

Although Lacey was recklessly overbearing, I was resigned that he was not a complete fool, so we were taking a risk that he might not fall for our trap. But soon his arrogance overcame his sense, and he completely disregarded the pact. Falling for the *Okie doke* quicker than expected, he removed Barry without an accord. Bonner was gone at the time so no one could tell him what to do. After all, he believed the long arms of The Buhl were cuddling him. Be that as it may, his foolish act of spite precipitated a series of clandestine meetings between our trio and some of the disgruntled air staff. The moment I'd delayed had finally come, and this was the honorable time to make a stand—all the key elements were now in place.

In Her Majesty's office, I introduced Kasuku and Bulldog as brothers in whom my confidence was well placed. I said that over time Kasuku had suggested that we take over the station, though I'd seen no way of doing it with the people we had on board. But now, as I'd told Kasuku, with the changing attitudes of the market and with some of the air staff (such as Moonman), we could pull it off as long as we got the anticipated help of the community. I then deferred to Kasuku.

"Though I've been walked through your situation, I need to ask a few questions," he began, remaining in his seat as he glanced at everyone present. "First of all, I'd like to ask Her Majesty what's her position?"

Her Majesty held no allegiance to Lacey – that much was sure. But in the past she was in Bonner's camp and uncomfortable with the views Kasuku represented. But she had changed. Now she said she'd go along with anything they planned as long as it made sense and there was no violence.

Kasuku pondered this in silence before looking around the group. He knew my primary reason for wanting to do this, but probed the others, "My question is why do y'all want to? Is it merely to enhance your pockets, your position and power? Somebody speak to that."

An uneasiness stirred about the room as people shifted in their seats. Then silence fell.

Her Majesty was troubled by the lack of response. She didn't want to take the lead again and appear to be hogging the show, as some would say Black women do "once they got their jaws flappin'." She waited this time, hoping someone else would express himself so she could judge what kind of thinking she had behind her. But as the silence dragged on, she had no choice but to take on the question.

"I suppose I can speak for all of us, Kasuku," she said. "Sure, we want position and power, but money is definitely not what's driving us. If it comes, that would only prove that our jobs were well done." She paused, looking at him sincerely, and continued, "We want to incorporate meaningful programs where the community can play an important part. We want to open the doors for others of color in this industry. The bottom line is all about putting brothers and sisters in power to give our community the respect and service it deserves. And we mean to do just that, no more."

"Will you alert the people about the dope that's infested our community? Will you get qualified people on the air to tell the truth about the situation?"

"Certainly, if we can find them," she said.

"Is that the way the rest of you feel?" Kasuku asked.

Silently, everyone approved, nodding his or her heads. Then he turned to me.

I said, "All we need to do now is bring the air staff together."

Moonman finally spoke up – the air staff was where he could help, and that's why he wanted to be here. Moonman was an ambitious young jock, two months on the job, who had impressed everyone with his mike presence and his aggressive style cutting good commercials. "We must bring The Tower down!" he said. "Lacey's causing nothing but trouble."

I tried to reassure Kasuku that my people were together, and I wanted support from him and his warriors. Kasuku was still weighing it, staring at Mitch in silence, trying to read the man in the three-piece suit before he turned back to me.

"Then let me get to the bottom line, little bruh," Kasuku said. "Are you sure y'all can handle y'all's end?"

I posed the question to each one, and every one agreed. Kasuku nodded his head slowly, gazing far away, deep in thought. Momentarily, he beckoned me as he and Bulldog stepped to the far end of the room where the others couldn't hear.

"They give all the right answers, but do you believe them?" he asked just above a whisper. "You know them, I don't. Plus are you sure there's no traitors among them? In other words, is *everythang everythang* in your eyes? I need to know that from you."

"Yeah, *everythang's everythang*. I wouldn't say so if I felt it wasn't."

"Sure, I know you wouldn't shit me. What you say, Bulldog?"

Bulldog nodded okay.

"Cool then, we're in. Touch base when y'all get y'all's *thang* together."

"Righ'On. Power to the people!" I responded.

Two days later, it became clear that someone must have leaked information to Lacey that enabled him to counter one of our moves. The finger seemed to point in the direction of the jocks, though we couldn't be sure whom.

Mitch and Her Majesty mulled it over in her office. She suggested setting a simple trap for each jock, something that only Mitch and she would know. Mitch was inclined to call a meeting to avoid someone copping an attitude for not being in on the know. But Her Majesty felt that they had to take the chance of going ahead themselves – they didn't have time. She knew the jocks' habits and knew exactly what to do. Besides she had already talked about it with me. So a different trap was set for each of the three jocks in question … only later to find Moonman-eating cheese with Lacey.

During the interrogation that followed at the next meeting, he was accused of being an Oreo, and Lacey's mole. Moonman lost it, attempting to defend his fragile integrity and tainted reputation. With his eyes staring from their sockets, his five-feet-five inch, two hundred thirty-five pound body shimmied each time he pounded the table. But no matter how vigorously he tried to intimidate us, his gibberish did nothing but aggravate his guilt. In the end, our words crushed him, and then we sent him summarily on his way.

With our suspicions put aside, the clock was ticking. It was now time to set the Struggle in motion. The team, including Kasuku, approached its task with analytical discernment. Along with citing the air staff's grievances, we agreed to put four demands to the Buhl: 1) that Barry be reinstated; 2) that Ted be appointed general manager; 3) that I be appointed General Sales Manager; 4) that an account be opened at the Black bank. Unwavering in our solidarity, the team came together with the handshake of self-determination to seal our resolve.

The following day, Friday, Mitch, Kasuku, Bulldog, and two outside union leaders took the grievances and demands to The Buhl. If no accord was reached, they would alert Ted and me, who were waiting at the Detroit Press Club to announce their grievances, and then a strike would be called.

In Mr. Beck's absence, Lacey and the two board members, Lawrence Roberts and Ed Butler, represented Beck on the other side of the table. Kasuku, in his African headgear and robe, read out the grievances and the demands.

"That's utter nonsense," Lacey barked, while the two board members looked apprehensively over their specs at Bulldog, who stood at ready when Lacey rose.

"We here are not racist," Lacey continued. "This station has devoted thirty-three years to the Negro community and has offered some of the earliest opportunities to Negro announcers. We have the right to choose whomever we please to be in management positions. Barry and Ted are just not qualified."

My name was also on the list of demands, so Mitch asked what about me?

"While he's an excellent salesman, he's not qualified either."

Mitch challenged Lacey to tell him what makes a person better qualified than hard work, credibility, an established record of sales, a rapport with people, and the respect of both business and local communities?

"What else does one need to be qualified?" Mitch pressed. "And what makes you so damn qualified—your fuckin' white skin? You know very little about the Black market, which you call Negro. The absurdity of your fuckin' comment is unmistakably clear. He pioneered the way for you and others, long before you came to this city. In other words, you're full of shit, man! And now you're saying none of these fuckin' demands will fly?"

Lacey snapped back that there was no need for that kind of

language. In regards to whether he'd grant any of the demands – absolutely not! Maybe the bank, but not the others. Lacey already wore those titles of general manager and general sales manager, and Moonman was his program director. "He's Black, ain't he?" Lacey taunted. "So how can you possibly call the company racist?"

"The company might or might not be racist," Kasuku countered calmly, "but you've just demonstrated its plantation mentality." He turned to the board members, "Do you two agree with him?"

Hardly taking their eyes off Bulldog, they nervously nodded affirmatively.

Sensing victory, Lacey lit into the two union leaders, "Christ, you two should know better than to be here. Those people are not even in a union. They're just disruptive elements talking about striking. That's what I call dumb! They have no case! I hold all the cards, and I'll use all of our resources to bring them down!"

"Then you're saying that's that?" Mitch concluded.

"You heard me."

As the silence stretched, Mitch picked up the phone situated at his side and called the Detroit Press Club. When he hung up, Kasuku rose. Then the group rose as one and filed out as planned.

CHAPTER FIFTEEN

Though only a scattering of press was on hand at the Detroit Press Club, Ted and I announced that The Buhl refused our grievances and demands. We made a statement of our resolve. And we called a strike. Immediately, we hurried back to The Tower. Out of thirty-two employees, eight in all were picketing outside.

Two of the jocks that we'd courted had joined up with Moonman and Lacey instead, who promised them a "bright future." Young, fresh up from the South, far from home in a big city swirling in racial conflicts, they were caught up in a world of confusion. All they wanted was simply a steady gig to survive and prove to their folks back home that they were hip enough to stay on the scene. Besides, where they had come from, no powerful, rich white men had ever capitulated under the demands of Negroes. It was too chancy to go along, so the hell with the Struggle; "Money talks, bullshit walks," and "the hand that pays the piper calls the tune." Unwittingly, they'd abandoned the real power that was tramping on the bricks outside, not realizing they were merely pawns of a woefully inadequate system, and had become adversaries to the strikers, just as Lacey and his lackeys were.

While the strikers persisted, Mitch and I left the line, rode up to the thirty-first floor and walked into the main studio. We brushed Motormouth aside, ignoring his objections, and seized the large, heavy carousel that contained the commercial cartridges, and lugged it down to our headquarters. A move out of desperation? Yes. But it was also a move to shut down the commercials and hit The Buhl in its pockets where it would hurt most. Nevertheless, our action was short lived. After Mitch called our attorney to bring him up to date, we begrudgingly returned the carousel, and rejoined Her Majesty, Ted, Gene, Barry and two other new jocks on the line.

As word of the strike got around The Tower, the staff grew uneasy. Lacey called The Buhl, and Butler ordered him to lock the lobby door and let no one out or in until the day was done.

The midday was fairly calm with a light breeze coming off the Detroit River nearby. In Grand Circle Park all the trees were lit up with colorful Christmas lights. And as the rides rolled by tooting their horns, the strikers waved their signs and shouted back, "Black Management for a Black Community." We picketed up to 6:00 PM, amusing ourselves with little jokes to relieve the strain of the day, and then retired to our headquarters. There, Mitch and I presided, discussing our intent and our agenda.

Mitch explained that we'd pulled the commercials as planned, but when the attorney said that was illegal, we had to return them. "I know it's a disappointment, but what can I say?"

I couldn't do anything about the commercials until the agencies opened, but come Monday, I'd be on them like white on rice to cancel their spots. In the meantime, I said they mustn't get discouraged because one plan went awry. We were the power representing the community's best interest, and we had the intellectual capital of our people. No one knew Lacey or his sidekicks. And The Buhl's influence in the community was tenuous at best.

"We have the power, y'all," I stressed. "And we have an agenda with so much more to do. We have to keep our faith, keep a clear head, stay strong, and press on."

Mitch told them I'd suggested our battle cry: "We Don't Want No Plantation Station." Over a hush of murmurs, he asked for any more suggestions.

Her Majesty said, "I think that describes our situation to a tee." In an exasperated voice she added, "It's close to 10 PM, y'all – let's get a consensus and call it a day, please."

The following morning, Saturday, everyone arrived on time with an optimistic outlook, which I found encouraging. Soon Kasuku and Bulldog joined us in the conference room. It was too early to hit the bricks, so we got busy assigning duties to cover all areas.

Mitch didn't want to use his offices to house the volunteers, especially since we didn't know what the turnout would be, so we decided to assemble them in the mezzanine.

"Now," Mitch said, holding a stogie as he read out the orders from a sheet before him. "Ted will be sequestered in my office. We want to keep him spotless from whatever might go down. And while he's there, we need him to compose a letter to solicit the support of the local unions, the city officials, the Black churches, every Black organization, most advertising agencies, and every Black business we have listed. When he's finished, Penelope and Her Majesty's workers, who are coming later, will type them up, make copies and send them out.

"Her Majesty has made arrangements to speak at several churches tomorrow. Gene will be on hand for the press at all times. Now, security: We'll need it for the building. Who'll help me take that on?"

I volunteered, but Mitch said, "No. you're supposed to keep order among the volunteers. Plus you got to call the advertisers, and you said you have several business meetings to address."

"No sweat, I can handle all of it," I said. "Besides, I have time between now and the meetings. If it's too much, I'll holler."

"Good enough," Mitch said. "Now, Barry, get the teen reporters together so they can round up some bodies for our Thursday rallies in Grand Circus Park. Do you need help?"

Barry said he could cover that, so Mitch turned the meeting over to me. I stood and smiled at everyone who was so enthusiastic this early Saturday morning. Then I introduced Kasuku and Bulldog for those who hadn't met them, describing them as long-time friends who, along with their warriors, would help in the Struggle. "They believe as I do that as a result of the Struggle and all the violations heaped upon our community that the community is ripe to stand behind our push. Most of you know where I'm coming from in terms of this whole *thang*. So for now, I'd like to defer to muh man, Kasuku."

"Power to the people!" Kasuku shouted, raising his clenched fist.

"Oh Lord," Her Majesty whimpered in surprise under her breath, having not faced the revolutionary side of Kasuku. And some of the others shifted uncomfortably in their seats.

"Power to the people!" Bulldog and I responded.

Kasuku understood that three jocks were lost, and he wanted to know if any others in this room believed the same as the three. If so, he wanted them to speak up now, or there would be some heartache if they were found out later. He was also concerned about press coverage, since there had been so little at our first press announcement.

Her Majesty knew they were guaranteed some coverage Wednesday in the Black press, but as far as the dailies, we'd just have to find a way of getting their attention.

Skeptical of the coverage we'd get from the white press, Kasuku left that in our hands. What concerned him more was the intellect of people on our own side. "Some of you might not know there's a revolution going on in here and out in the streets." Determined that his words were heard, he intoned, "I want all of you to know that I don't fall in line with just anyone or anything." He paused to take stock of those present, and said it was for me and for the cause. "I consider it a privilege to commit myself and my warriors. We're joining in your Struggle to put a revolutionary spin on it. My warriors and I can help greatly through intimidation and threats. If you all want us to go further by breaking limbs or blowing up The Tower's transmitter, we're prepared to do so. It depends on you. What do you want?"

"Please, we don't want to use any violence," Her Majesty called out. "We're not against the employees, just Lacey and this lousy system. What do the rest of you say?"

I said, "we're all in agreement with you, dear." But I looked at Kasuku seriously and added, "Other than violence, do whatever is necessary. When can you start?"

"Give me a list of names, phone numbers, and addresses of all the employees including the owner, and we'll start tonight."

"Righ'On," I smiled and thanked Kasuku for supporting us. I went on that I too had concerns about getting press because Beck and his family had a real vested interest there. To counter that, we'd need to use all our influence to get the news of our Struggle out. Each of us had to call every chatterbox we knew to help pass the word. Second, we all had to contribute a small donation to get our Struggle off the ground. "As much as we can, we'll use Her Majesty's ministerial expertise in begging," I added, and paused to allow the laughter to subside over her mild objections.

I said Gene and Barry would supply food, first-aid kits and walkie-talkies. Her Majesty's workers would get volunteers to inundate The Tower and The Buhl with inquiries. Barry would also get bullhorns for the rallies in Grand Circus Park, and Gene would arrange for more material for picket signs. We all knew the drill. All that was left to do was preserve our faith and hold firm. "So let's stay strong!"

On the picket line, the strikers talked to everyone who seemed to be curious, taking the opportunity to explain our position and asking them to pass on the word. To our pleasure, a few people dropped what they were doing and joined the volunteers, relieving us on line. As the day moved on, the mezzanine became a rest and comfort spot, and the picket line stayed moderately strong well into the evening. As we'd do each night, the strikers retired to our headquarters to critique the day's experiences. Afterward, in solidarity, we bowed our heads, hands together, in prayer.

"We believe. We know. We thank You, Father."

On Sunday. I was awakened by the trumpet sounds of a neighbor's car alarm. A crook in my neck snapped as I unraveled my torso from the armchair on which I'd fallen asleep. I looked out the window. Quiet – not even footprints in the light snow that had fallen during the mid-December night. My watch showed 7:25, earlier than I would have wakened, but I shrugged and considered the incident a wake-up call. Soon I was out of my crib, negotiating the four miles of the nearly empty freeway, anxious about the events of the day to come.

Two grassroots brothers, whom I'd been mentoring in the fundamentals of selling the Black market, joined in the picket line. Everyone walked in a circle outside the entrance, wearing away the fresh snow beneath our feet. The weather was brisk. And each time we passed each other in the circle, someone tossed out some down-home phrase from a time long past to plump up our strength and encouragement for the hours ahead.

The barbs and laughter flowed back and forth for most of the morning. A long-time advertiser brought us headgear and gloves. The Flaming Embers offered us free lunches and dinners. Over the course of the day, we were joined by at least seventy people representing every facet of the community from the Black Panthers to the NAACP. On top of that, several record promoters came out bringing coffee, sodas, and money. Most of the other folks just came to extend good will and lend their bodies to the picket line. We gave each of them the phone numbers of The Tower and The Buhl to call and make inquiries. The word was getting out. But still no press.

That evening when I was in the main lobby, I received an alert on my walkie-talkie. Immediately, I cautioned Tina, who was the only elevator operator on at the time. Tina was in the strikers' corner so I counted on her not to allow a certain person up until I had a chance to engage him. I beckoned to Mitch, who was picketing outside, to join me. We stood out of sight behind an alcove forty feet from the back. Tina stood nearby, just around the corner.

"It's Moonman. He's sneaking in from the back," she whispered.

"Okay," I said. "Step to the operator's desk where we can see you. When he gets to the elevator, scratch your head; then we'll come out."

Moonman walked cautiously toward the elevator. The coast was clear; no one around but Tina. Just as he was about to step into the elevator, Tina scratched her head, and Mitch and I stepped out into the open. Moonman was stunned! He froze momentarily in wide-eyed fright before he quickly jumped into the elevator and pulled the lever to ascend.

In that instant, Tina hit the main switch at the operator's desk, stopping the elevator and opening its door. There stood Moonman, halfway up the door. It was a funny sight, with only his legs and feet showing. While his feet shuffled from one side of the elevator to the other, Mitch and I burst out laughing.

"Let's break his fuckin' kneecaps! Get that long iron bar outside the door," Mitch ordered me while winking at Tina.

"Oh please, don't break his legs," Tina pleaded, going along with the program.

"No, the traitor got it coming. We don't need him or anyone like him around. He's a disgrace to all Black folks."

From the back of the elevator, Moonman could only see us from our shoulders up. Helpless, he couldn't discern why he was in this fix. Yes, he had sided with Lacey, but he felt that was his right to choose if he was the better man for the job than Barry. At least that's what Lacey had told him often enough. Why couldn't the others see that, Moonman wondered. He hadn't done any more than some of the others would have done to advance their career, he thought, never figuring that his cocky, youthful ego had gotten in the way of realizing that Lacey only wanted a gullible person of color to parrot his words. But when he heard the iron bang on the stone floor, his thoughts abruptly escaped him.

"This ought to do the job," Mitch said, raising and sliding the bar on the elevator's floor.

"You're not really going to do that, are you?" Tina questioned.

"Sure, why not?" Then he told me to get the small table behind the back door so he could stand on it and have the proper angle to get to his knees.

Moonman wasn't about to be incapacitated without resisting. He tried to grab hold of the bar. But each time Mitch saw his hands reach down for it, he pulled it away and poked at his legs. The elevator rumbled as Moonman shook in his shoes.

Mitch put the table back in place and winked at Tina again.

"Mitch, don't do it. Please don't do it," she cried out.

"I must teach this Oreo a lesson, Tina. Get back, get back."

"No, I'll have to call the police, and you'll get in more trouble than it's worth. You talk to him," she pleaded to me. "Make him see it doesn't make any sense."

"She's right," I said. "That'll take you away from our Struggle and we can't afford that, muh man. So bring him down. At least he won't be doing his show today."

"Okay, Tina, bring him down and get him the hell out of here before I change my mind."

Later that evening, while the strikers were having our usual pow-wow, Mitch announced that our attorney had called and informed him that The Buhl had filed a suit in the Wayne County Circuit Court charging us with harassing and assaulting non-striking personnel and pressuring businesses to withdraw their advertisements.

"But he also said not to be too concerned about it. Just don't do anything that might be considered illegal," Mitch quickly added to soothe everyone's anxieties.

Minutes later, Arthur, the night man, burst into the conference room. "There're policemen downstairs!" he yelled breathlessly. "They said they're here to search this building."

"For what?" Mitch asked, but Arthur didn't know.

Mitch told everyone to sit tight as he and I took care of it. He picked up his stogie, and the two of us scurried off with Arthur to the elevator. When its door opened on the main floor, we beheld a sergeant and two patrolmen standing with arms folded.

"What's the problem?" Mitch asked, puffing hard on the stogie, emitting clouds of smoke.

"We need to go to the thirty-first floor. We understand there's been trouble up there," the sergeant declared with authority as he puffed out his chest while pulling up his pants.

"There's no trouble up there. As you can see, there's a strike taking place."

"Yes, I can see. Still, I need to go up and check things out."

By now, some of the volunteers were curious. They came in and crowded around. The two patrolmen were getting fidgety, their eyes shifting from the volunteers to the sergeant.

"Stop crowding around here," the sergeant ordered. "Get back outside!"

"Stay put!" Mitch barked.

"Who are you?"

"I manage this building," he said, the stogie fixed between his lips. "And unless you can show me a fuckin' search warrant, you'd better leave this building now."

"Show me some proof," the sergeant said.

Taking the stogie from his mouth, Mitch said, "I don't have to show you a damn thing but that revolving door."

"Righ'On," the volunteers called out.

The sergeant's face was turning red as he backed away, pulling the two officers aside. Only their mumbling could be heard, but judging by their gestures it was clear that the two were at odds with the sergeant. Then one of the patrolmen turned his back and walked away. In a moment, the other followed.

"You win this round, but I'll be back, ya hear!" the sergeant vowed.

It was the first time many of the volunteers had witnessed their long-time archenemies on the defense and finally backing down. The scene manifested a real sense of empowerment in them, something they had never felt before in the presence of white police. Some smiled, some laughed, then they all cheered and gave up some skin to one another, as the police filed through the revolving door.

On a chilly Monday, our battle cry, "We don't want no plantation station" reverberated across the street and into the park, drawing more curiosity seekers into our fold. The turnout crammed and overflowed the mezzanine, and picketers with their signs, seeking refuge from the cold, lined the congested main lobby.

It was the first full working day for the building's mostly white tenants who were doctors, lawyers, gold and silver brokers, dental suppliers, entrepreneurs, and other professionals. Their reactions varied. Those who were not aware of the strike were taken aback by what appeared to be its suddenness. Others entered with scorn on their faces, bitter and frustrated, mostly concerned about their clientele's reactions and their business address getting negative exposure.

Through the morning, I made calls to my clients and to other advertisers. Wary of alienating them, I took the soft sell approach. I didn't solicit a cancellation or a stop directly, but apprised them with first hand information so, if they chose, they could make their own decisions, well-informed about the facts, and so the agencies could alert their clients and discuss their questions intelligently. Though the process was arduous, it went smoothly enough with those I found in their offices; I'd call the others back. It wasn't until I joined Mitch in the main lobby downstairs, that I saw the congestion there.

"How did it go," Mitch asked, worried.

"So far, so good. Whether they'll cancel remains up in the air." I was distracted, looking around. "I see we really got a mess on our hands here."

Mitch thought he had a solution to this mob, which would also solve another problem concerning the jocks on the air. The jocks weren't crossing our picket line, and they weren't coming in through the back door. Yet they were on the air, so they were getting in somehow, or sleeping in. So Mitch thought of moving the volunteers up to the tenth floor when they were on breaks from walking the line, which would give us more space downstairs. And if the jocks were getting in from the back, somehow, they'd be able to tell.

So the volunteers were moved up to a suite on the tenth floor that overlooked the back area below. A lookout equipped with a walkie-talkie was posted at a window there an hour prior to each show change. If a jock was seen sneaking up the ally, I would be alerted by walkie-talkie. But I found no jock coming though the back lobby door to confront. Yet, in no time, he was heard conducting his show. How did he get in?

That remained an enigma until Tina discovered the jocks were entering through the outer back door. They sneaked from there to the basement where they took the freight elevator, not visible from the lobby, to the mezzanine. There, they switched to one of the regular elevators to take them up to The Tower.

So on the next call my crew and I gathered in the dark space between the lobby's door and the outer door. Huddled in a way that concealed us from the shaft of light that would strike when the door was opened, we waited.

"Shhh," I cautioned when I heard someone outside the back door. The jock entered. He hit the light switch and suddenly found himself surrounded by menacing eyes of unfamiliar, hardened faces.

"Let's get him," someone in my crew cried out.

The shock and fright that registered across the jock's face was clearly enough to make a weak man mess his pants. He pleaded for mercy, then covered his head with his arms and commenced to bob and weave to ward off the anticipated blows.

"Why shouldn't we kick your ass and break your fuckin' legs for crossing the line, you Oreo," someone else in the crew taunted, moving forward. But he stopped on my command.

"It's my job, man," the jock sobbed. "I can't afford to lose it. I got responsibilities, a wife and two kids back home to support. If not, I'd be out there with y'all. Y'all gotta believe me, hear?"

I let him go with a warning: "If we catch your behind out here again we're gonna break both your legs for real."

"Yes sir. Yes sir. You won't see me again, I promise."

It was a pitiful sight to see a grown man frightened to this point, and I figured the jock's heart had skipped enough beats. As the crew and I started for the inner lobby door, I turned and saw the jock bend to his knees, and I could only imagine he was giving thanks to his savior for bringing him out unharmed.

Tuesday was an upbeat day. The weather had cleared and the sun was out. Telegrams from members of congress, union officials, councilmen and women, businesspeople, community activists, and members of the clergy were displayed across the conference table.

Then came word that many of the office staff didn't show up, leaving The Tower in a sorry plight. The inquiring calls and cancellations that inundated its switchboard were too much for the lean staff to process. And one of our big goals became a reality: all commercials were pulled. There was no talk, no public service announcements, no nothing but music and station identification breaks. This turn of events was far more than we'd dared to hope so soon. God had answered our prayers. Now all that was lacking was press coverage, and a call from The Buhl.

The Buhl board members were panicked. They had followed Lacey's lead, never expecting the strike to go as long as it had, and were desperate for ways to turn the morass in their favor.

To temper the board's anxieties, Lacey had abandoned The Tower and he and Moonman set up an office at The Buhl. Away from the fray, Lacey thought he'd figured out a way to mobilize public opinion against the strikers.

"Okay," he told the Board, "so we ran into a little snag, but I think I know what's happening. Listen, and see if you agree, Moonman. I don't believe the community really knows what's going on here. What do you say about that?"

"I agree. I was seriously thinking just that. I believe if it really knew, we'd get its support."

"How do you plan to get its support?" Ed Butler asked, nervous and still undecided.

Lacey responded that it was easy enough. He still had several cards to play, and they could use their facilities to fight fire with fire. He'd write an editorial and air it every fifteen minutes tomorrow. It would be a piece of cake if done correctly, and he had no doubt he'd do it perfectly. They'd be back in business before the week was out. "How does that sound?" he said. "Can I get a vote on it?"

Since all else had failed, and no one offered an alternative, all thumbs went up.

On returning to my crib earlier than usual that evening, I received a call from my mole at The Tower. She told me of a conversation she'd had with Moonman, where she learned that Lacey would make his counter attack tomorrow. She didn't know what or how because Moonman wouldn't tell her, but look for something big.

I hardly gave her warning a second thought. After all, what could Lacey do? We had reviewed all possibilities and had our bases covered.

Early Wednesday, Lacey sat comfortably with Moonman in Studio B and recorded his editorial:

"It is with regret and a deep sense of concern over the events of the past four days of violence, hate and intimidation, plus an even greater concern over the safety of our employees, that ownership and management of radio station WTOP presents this editorial..."

Lacey went on to contend that for many years WTOP had been dedicated to service to the Black community, and then he continued:

"Unbelievable conditions have existed at WTOP. We have been truly under siege. The lives of our employees have been violently threatened. Threats against the wives of our Black employees have been so severe that WTOP has moved employees from their homes to hidden locations throughout the city, changing these locations from time to time to protect their safety...

"It was necessary to hire a battery of armed private guards to protect the lives of our people and our property. An engineer's pregnant and terrified wife was told on the phone that her baby would not be born alive... One of three jocks' wives was told that her husband was about to be dropped in the Detroit River. Another was told not only her husband but she would also die...

"Our traffic manager, who courageously came to work in spite of vile and obscene threats at her home and at the station, was scared out of her wits. Everyone here, including my wife and I, has been threatened. Men were even stationed in and behind our building and on nearby corners equipped with walkie-talkies, making reports on movements into or near our building by our faithful employees. Armed guards were assigned to protect WTOP's transmitter in Highland Park, which was also threatened. Many of WTOP's Black and white employees phoned in ill rather than risk entering our building. Full police protection was demanded for our people. Police answered a bomb threat, which had been phoned to our central office. Fifteen minutes later, we received a similar bomb threat at WTOP studios. This frantic cloud of brutality and these violent threats continue to hang over WTOP. Yesterday the intimidation continued, only now it was directed toward our advertisers. Scores of WTOP advertisers who have already canceled their announcements and programs on our station have expressed their support but were fearful for their lives and business…

"What you're hearing may sound like make believe to you. But let me assure you that to those of us who have lived through these past days, it has not been make believe. Have we really reached the point in our history that the alternative to working together is violence, hate, and total destruction of our system? As bad as it may be, can't we work together to make it as good as we can? All of us at WTOP believe that there are men and women in our community who deplore violence, hate and brutal intimidation. We believe you far outnumber those who advocate the tactics of terror. These tactics are designed to have WTOP give in completely to demands without compromise, or to put WTOP off the air. Those of us who are still here shall do neither. WTOP shall continue to dedicate itself to the Black Americans of Detroit. Help us overcome the evils of hate. We need your support. If you believe as we believe, write us! Wire us! Phone us! WTOP Detroit."

Those of us who knew the actual facts knew that Lacey's piece was so exaggerated it was bizarre. Yet it was so well done it occurred to me that speech classes across the country could use it to teach students the many tricks and ploys of public speaking. Lacey's delivery was exceptional with proper inflections punctuating specific words. In moments, his voice became beautifully emotional, righteously indignant, benignly innocent and incredulous that the strikers had him against the wall.

Back in the studio as the tape rewound, Lacey and Moonman bobbed their heads in agreement, smirking with satisfaction. "I think this should light a huge bonfire," Lacey said smugly, handing the tape to Moonman to run it on the quarter hour. Eagerly anticipating the reaction, he bet Moonman I would shit in my pants, "and Her Majesty will have a baby."

Meanwhile, I was in the midst of a witty speech at a business luncheon, the type of setting where business politicking was part of the purpose. Because of my profession, my various speeches, and my social activism, I was well known. Dressed in a black dashiki with a bright print pattern complimented by a black silk turtleneck shirt with sleeves bloused above the cuffs, black bell-bottom pants, shiny black kicks, a gleaming gold pendant hanging from a gold chain on my chest, and matching cufflinks that shined with each movement of my hands, I had made absolutely sure nothing about me would cause me any sense of insecurity.

Though my dress and address was conspicuously different from most members of this audience of two hundred mostly middle-aged, conservative business and public relations people, and even though most of them were entrenched in their complacency, they nevertheless listened intensely.

Hoping to arouse their concern, I soon dropped the witticisms. Standing tall, I refreshed their memory of past times – Rosa Parks, SCLC marches, CORE's Freedom Rides, and SNCC's sit-ins and voter registration. I invoked the Algiers Motel slaying, the League of Revolutionary Black Workers, and the Republic of New Africa–New Bethel Church fiasco to bring my point closer to home.

I spoke of the attitudes that people held in the hope that those present could and would identify themselves with one or more of the sentiments. I spoke about change to those who would reject changes of any kind which might affect their status, their habits or their environment, and who saw change as distant and slow, something that happened without any stimulus. I spoke of those who acted with patronizing indifference and those who lived in denial. And I spoke of those who, on the other hand, demanded radical changes "by any means necessary" without prudent planning.

Finally I was ready to veer to the Struggle at WTOP, describing exactly how it had come about and what the strike was expected to resolve. Then, as an addendum, I appealed to them:

"The people of this city have served as vanguards in the Afro-American Struggle, and are still playing their part in this nation's revolution, a people's revolution that has caused many to act and react in ways they'd never before dreamed. It's a people's revolution that has stimulated relevant communication where none had existed before. It's a revolution, too, that has brought to the forefront many courageously strong and compassionate hearts, which, through their collective protest-demonstrations and marches, are moving this nation toward changes for the betterment of all mankind.

"As in this city and nation, there's a revolution going on at WTOP as well. I now ask your support for the strikers there."

The spirit had hit me. I was feeling its momentum, and I wanted to carry on. But I knew, like any good speaker would know, I'd made my point. After all, the audience's main priority was getting a piece of the pie. So I left a thought-provoking query for each one there: "In the greater scheme of things, do you really care about the revolution? Or will you wait until the next long hot summer comes, then volunteer to give your postmortem appraisal?"

As I left the podium, the group rose in applause, probably at my candor. I took solace in the moment, my spirits glowing from the group's uninhibited approval that was an affirmation of my mission accomplished.

Returning to my crib to switch gears, I changed into my poor-man suit, and left to pick up Kasuku.

CHAPTER SIXTEEN

After hearing the editorial, Her Majesty and Mitch looked at one another in disbelief.

"Was I hearing right? Was that supposed to be us?" she exclaimed.

"I suppose so. We're the only ones striking here."

The editorial was a bit too much for Her Majesty to handle, let alone deal with how some of the listeners would react. Our attorney had said the suit The Buhl filed Tuesday should be coming up soon, and Her Majesty figured the broadcast would go against us in court. But Mitch cautioned her not to jump to conclusions and sit tight until I arrived with the real low down on Kasuku's actions.

They didn't have to wait long. The moment Kasuku and I stepped into the conference room, Her Majesty asked, "Have you two been listening to the station?"

"Yes, we heard the editorial, if that's what you mean. By the tone of it, Kasuku and his warriors have been doing a bang-up job for us, wouldn't you say?" I smiled in jest. She didn't take it as the least bit funny, so I went on, "Look, as far as my part, I know what my approach was to the agencies. Believe me, it was nothing like what Lacey described. The editorial is unbelievable – a red herring full of sanctimonious hyperboles to undermine our credibility in our community."

"He's right," Kasuku said.

"Then you didn't do all that – like he said, it was exaggerated," Her Majesty prompted Kasuku for assurance.

Actually, what I'd said was correct... up to a point. Kasuku reminded them that he was a revolutionist. He thought revolution, and we'd given him the green light to practice his craft. But, as I'd mentioned, the piece was embellished beyond reason.

"It was a beautiful, real live tear-jerker, all right," Mitch noted. "Lacey pulled out all stops and reached out and grabbed everything he could lay his fuckin' hands on to solicit sympathy."

"Regardless, do y'all think Lacey's trick will work?" Her Majesty asked.

"I doubt it," Mitch responded.

I'd heard the phrase, "truth is the first casualty of war," and now it had come home. I reminded them our struggle was a result of Lacey's heavy-handedness, as well as an indictment against a woefully inadequate system. We knew hate was not our *thang*. Our goal, which was fair from the start, was to gain a relevant voice for our community. Striking in the cold of winter, just before Christmas, was an inconvenience for our families as well as ourselves, but we had faith in our cause, and it had to be done.

"Long before our run-in," I continued, "I tried to get through to Lacey that Black folks' attitudes were very different from those of Negroes on important issues. But my remarks never sunk in. All Lacey seemed to conclude was that he, rather than Mr. Beck, was the Massa of the plantation. And as Massa, he would deal with as heavy hand as all other Massas had done before him. Obviously, to Lacey, this strike was a revolt, the nearest thing to war. And as in a war, he did what he felt he had to do. He took his best shot for his own survival."

"But what he don't know," Kasuku injected, "is that our community has far too long been seduced by the Colgate smile, and the 'I'm-doing-you-a-big-favor' attitude of his kind. And I don't think the community will take it on their knees."

Still worried, Her Majesty said, "Where do we go from here?"

"We can't afford to rush to judgment," I said. "Let's see what the response will be; then we can hammer out our strategy and press on."

Nothing but good sprang from the editorial. Lacey's provocative smokescreen backfired in the Black community. It gave the Struggle more exposure to the right ears than any other means could. Abetted by the story in the weekly Black *Detroit Chronicle*, the news of the strike spread like wild flowers.

Everyone in the community was talking about it: "Who is this Lacey person, anyway? How can a radio station on the thirty-first floor of a public building in the heart of downtown Detroit, with hundreds of others operating in that building, be placed under siege? What gives Lacey the right to vilify the strikers who had always worked for the good of the total community? Had the Black staff, within a few days, suddenly become skilled in guerilla warfare?"

Thursday: Lacey's major flaw was that he had no inkling of the temperament of the community. That's why his editorial backfired and galvanized a ground swell of grass roots supporters from the community. In fact, the strikers had never before witnessed a better example of media power! Awash with volunteers, over two hundred spirited backers came by buses, in their rides, in cabs, and some of the hippies I'd met on Plum Street came on foot to join in. A few dudes off the street were hoping to be in the thick of what they'd thought was a raging battle, only to be met with disappointment. Nevertheless, most people suspected the editorial's deceit and came clamoring for change. A gush of excitement filled the air.

Six strikers, three mediators and Kasuku sat around the conference table. Two other strikers were downstairs on the line giving directions to the volunteers, while Her Majesty's workers kept order on the tenth floor. We decided we had enough volunteers on hand to allow us to expand our protest and hit closer to the heart of the company. What we came up with was picketing Beck's residence in Grosse Point Shores, as well as picketing The Buhl to put direct pressure on them.

"If one of you comes along," Kasuku said, "me and some of my warriors will go out to Beck's home."

Mitch looked around the table, and chose. "Gene, you still need to be available for the press. Barry has to take care of the rally in the park. Billy, you go along with Kasuku." Then Mitch turned to me, "We'll go over to The Buhl, all right?"

Kasuku piled his crew into two rides and left. Mitch and I formed our crew and left also, leaving a dense line of protesters picketing The Tower. We paraded down Woodward Avenue on our way to The Buhl, raising our fists and signs to everyone we passed – the Hare Krishnas, the Black Panthers, and the Black Muslims, all hawking their magazines and newspapers along the way. Upon arriving at The Buhl, we chanted our war cry with full-throated voices, which carried up between the skyscrapers to the twentieth floor where The Buhl, now aware of the backlash, had been in a tactical meeting all morning.

Upstairs, Butler was speaking when a clerk, just back from a break, burst through the door unannounced and cried out that they're downstairs picketing us!

"What?" Butler howled, pushing his glasses up on his nose. "Who's downstairs?"

The clerk told him that Mitch and I headed the picketers and the twenty of us were attracting a lot of attention.

"Call the police."

"They're already down there, doing nothing, just sitting in their cruisers."

Lacey rushed to the window nearest to him and cracked it open. A gush of chilly wind charged through the room.

"Can you see anything?" Butler asked, his arms folded around his chest to ward off the chill.

"No, it's too sharp an angle. But I can see across the street that some people and the police are looking toward this building," he remarked as he slammed the window closed.

The men shook off their chill and looked at one another, bewildered. Suddenly the phone punctured the silence, startling them. Butler picked it up. After several minutes of silence on his end, he said "Thanks," then rested the receiver. It was the building management confirming what they already knew. He sighed, then looked to their attorney and demanded, "When does our court hearing come up? How long will it take to stop this! When will all this end?"

The attorney tried to placate Butler, "I took it to a judge I know. I imagine not too long – maybe today or tomorrow at the latest."

Meanwhile, on the street, the protesters shouted our war cries for a couple of hours, "Black Management for a Black Community," and "We Don't Want No Plantation Station."

When we returned to The Tower, I found Kasuku and his crew on the picket line.

"How did it go, muh man," I asked.

"No sooner did we start picketing Beck's home, the police arrived and ordered us off his property. All I can say is that his neighbors and his family knew we were out there," he shrugged, disappointment showing in his eyes.

Later that afternoon, Judge Dalton Harvey, a heavy set man with a disillusioned, jowly face issued his ruling to the attorneys for the company and the strikers. Judge Harvey had once been considered a conservative, but lately he'd made some liberal rulings so no one was sure what he'd do in this case.

"...And a man's home is his castle," he expounded. "The strikers cannot threaten the safety of a person's family because of a business dispute. I order the strikers to cease harassing the employees and to cease the picketing of Mr. Beck's home. As for The Tower and The Buhl, they are free to do so."

For The Buhl, it was a bittersweet ruling. They had gotten some satisfaction, but it left their major concern still up in the air. They couldn't resume the ad spots for lack of personnel. They were losing money by the hour, and there seemed to be no ending in sight. Moreover, having picketers outside their doors was embarrassing and an affront to the proud Beck's name. The situation looked grim, and the ground was shaking under Lacey.

Showing much strain and exhaustion, Butler rose. "This whole ordeal," he said, "is not helping Mr. Beck get any better on his sick bed. He wants this thing brought to an end! Whatever we come up with this time must be final, or I'm afraid some of us won't be around."

Lacey believed the community's reaction was an anomaly. But he admitted it was too late for damage control. They'd better lick their wounds and move on. "Why not pretend to bite the bullet, and give them a hollow victory," Lacey said. "If we can get the strikers off the street and away from the people, we'll have a better chance to control this whole situation quietly. I have some things in mind." He looked to his parrot, "Moonman, what do you think?"

"I agree—it's an anomaly. The community has given them unexpected support. As you said, take that support away, then the momentum swings to our side."

"I hope this plan is better than your last one," Butler said, his face pale and haggard. "So, what do you have?"

"Okay, we'll give them a hollow victory. Then we'll..."

Almost an hour later, we received a call from our attorney. The Buhl was ready to talk! We gathered with our mediators, three top Black union leaders, a community activist, and a writer from the weekly Black *Detroit Chronicle*. Deliberating on the grievances and demands we added: 1) the removal of Moonman from The Tower's premises; 2) that there be no retaliation against any strike participant; 3) that all court charges be dropped, and 4) that there be retroactive pay for all time lost by the employees because of the strike.

Friday: The mediators took our request to The Buhl, and returned later with the agreement all signed, sealed and delivered.

One of the union leaders said, "This agreement looks good. It gives you all you'd asked for. But I don't like the way it went down. Lacey and the others seemed a little too content. I'd suggest you all start working on a contingency plan."

With this in mind, we all locked hands in prayer.

"...We believe. We know. We thank You Father."

CHAPTER SEVENTEEN

The first day back was hectic. The disarray of files and logs clearly spoke to the confusion that had occurred. There were make-goods to be rescheduled and logged, cancellations to be submitted, and copies to be revised, not to mention the calls to clients to update them on the outcome.

As might be expected, The Tower's workload stressed relationships that had already been strained. Although most of our co-workers understood the reason for the strike, coming back together taxed the tolerance of some of them. Mistakes were made and tempers flared as the problems mounted.

According to the strike agreement, Ted was named General Manager, cloaked with complete authority to control operations of The Tower, subject only to veto powers of Mr. Beck or Mr. Roberts, whom the strikers trusted more than Butler. But despite the legal settlement, Ted was locked out of both the general manager's office and the filing cabinets containing the business records. After Ted had keys made for both, Mr. Roberts threatened to demote him, and ordered him to move from the front office to a small one at the back of the station. There he was left to sit at a clerical desk deprived of anything with which to work.

Ted recommended that the credit manager, an ally of Lacey's, be dismissed for coming on the job intoxicated, refusing to work, and disappearing for three days after stating that he "quit," but Ted was ignored. And his efforts to make some operational changes at The Tower were discounted once Lacey assumed the title of Managing Director over Ted.

Moonman, who had supposedly been barred from the premises, was in and out, interfering with the air staff's assignments and music selections. He proclaimed that he was now the newly appointed National Program Director, and with that title, he had authority to hire and fire all air staff personnel.

So at the end of a week of protracted negotiations, the strikers hadn't gotten off the mark. Since Mr. Beck was ill, and Mr. Roberts, his designee, knew nothing about how to manage The Tower, Lacey's sinister plot became evident. Conducting the covert action was symptomatic of Lacey's character. Obviously, he had no intention of honoring the agreement and had chosen to continue the Struggle inside The Tower, away from the street scene and the probing eyes and ears of the community. We were also convinced that Lacey believed we might have won the scrimmage but certainly not the Struggle. Since he thought no one could outwit him, he never suspected that we had a strategy. In fact, we'd devised a plan this time, which would bring us instantaneous response from the community and the press.

And I was more determined than ever to break Lacey. It was time to make my last ditch effort to bring some sanity to The Tower.

I'd been raised to believe that if I had a problem I should go to the main source of it. I reasoned Butler was that source. I knew he had no moxie and believed he was a paper tiger, so a meeting with him would be my course of action. I wasn't interested in dethroning Butler, only convincing him that, even under the present circumstances, he had no need to fear me. It was all about what would soon be beneficial for both the company and the community. But if all didn't go well, being the poker player that I was, I knew the value of having an ace in the hole. I had one. And if necessary, I'd uncover it, leaving Butler no wiggle room, forcing him to follow through on my demands.

Butler must have thought it was peculiar when I called. It had been quite some time since we'd last met, and Butler probably expected that I was open to make some kind of deal. Far from our previous collaborations, Butler now viewed me as a Black militant and was leery of me. Still, he was curious enough to meet.

We came together at the usual place, with apprehension on both sides of the table. I wasted little time getting to the crux of the problem. I hammered away at Lacey and Moonman's so-called new positions. I wanted them out. Those new titles existed only to undermine the strikers' deal even at the risk of putting The Tower's functions and its bottom line in jeopardy. What could be more important to an accountant than that? Nonetheless, my argument seemed not to have made the least bit of an impression.

To Butler, I was untrustworthy. Since the strike, he had come to believe Lacey's derogatory remarks were all true and I was the real enemy. Butler wanted no part of me.

On the other side of the table, I was sensing all the bad vibes. I could see by Butler's posture that he'd been taken in by Lacey's slander. Or maybe that defensive body language was an effect of the taxing strike. In any case, Butler was jumpy, suspicious and unfocused. Regardless, I was determined to be heard – that's what I'd come for. After wrestling for two hours, Butler and I were still like two drunkards, not sure of our footing, stumbling along a road that led to nowhere. In spite of that, before we parted, I was resolute: I wanted both Lacey and Moonman gone from The Tower. I needed an answer today, not tomorrow. "So, what's up?" I challenged him.

Nothing was up. After all the years, Butler was still in Mr. Beck's corner. Whatever Mr. Beck wanted, he got. And Lacey was Beck's man. What more could Butler say?

Butler had said enough, and I didn't like the answer. As we got up to leave, the time had come for me to take off the gloves and prove I was a force to be reckoned with.

Outside, I beckoned Butler to accompany me to my ride. There was something very important there I wanted to put on his mind. Whatever it was, Butler had made up his mind not to fall prey to my cause. When we were both seated, I reached across Butler, popped open the glove compartment, retrieved a small package, and opened it to reveal my wild card. I told Butler to get comfortable and listen closely as I placed the Silencer on the dashboard. I turned up the volume and pushed the on switch.

Hearing the date and time didn't mean anything to Butler at first. But when he heard himself in conversation with me, he had a rude awakening. The bittersweet memories of that day and night came rushing back. He choked. I smelled blood. I imposed an ultimatum: Either Butler pulled the two from The Tower by the end of the week or I would send out copies not only to Mr. Beck, but also to every station the company owned in and out of town.

"Think of the humiliation for you and your family, and the possibility of you losing your position. It's nothing personal, just business. Need I say more?" I said with blank finality.

Later that day, I called the strikers together. Without mentioning my episode with Butler, the strikers and I discussed our position thoroughly. It was decided that we had tried everything in good faith. And it was clear that the agreement was a ruse. So we had news for them—it was crunch time. Tomorrow, we'd have no choice but to implement our plan.

The following morning at 11:50, eight days before Christmas, we locked the doors to the lobby and barricaded the entire glass front with some of its furniture. The strikers and most of our co-workers sat peacefully on the floor. At twelve noon, Her Majesty got into the segment of her show that had most listeners. That's when show time began.

Her voice, weary with consternation and dismay, cracked as she struck a match at the microphone. The match popped and reverberated through the airwaves. She struck another in succession. It popped! She screamed! The audio went mute.

Instantly, the phone lines lit up as we sat ignoring them. Five minutes, then ten minutes, then eleven minutes passed. At 12:18 PM, eight policemen and a fire rescue squad, reporters and photographers from each daily, and others from the community presses were crowding the outer lobby. Her Majesty's listeners, thinking she had been shot, as we expected they would, had called everybody to the rescue. Not until the police witnessed her strolling through the lobby were they convinced she'd met no harm. They left; so did the rescue squad. Only the press lingered, hollering though the glass front, bent on getting a story.

"We're off the air until this thing is over!" the strikers shouted to the press.

"What thing?"

The strikers let the question hang before referring the reporters to our attorney, Samuel Goodman, who was in court representing us.

Actually, most of the strikers had never met Mr. Goodman, so they were intrigued when a large dark complexioned white man with the rugged face of an old sailor arrived, radiating excitement. His deep base voice commanded immediate attention.

"I know how anxious you all must be," he began. "We were in court for only about a half hour. I told the judge what had transpired, and then told him the agreement was a rosy-red apple full of worms. After our adversary spoke on behalf of The Buhl's conduct, the judge agreed that they had not bargained in good faith. He ordered them to cease and to carry out the agreement as ordered."

"Need I ask how The Buhl took it?" Her Majesty smiled, anticipating more pleasure.

"I can say joyously that their lawyer told me that Mr. Butler had recanted his position."

"Did he tell you why Butler flip-flopped?" Her Majesty said.

Goodman didn't know. He could only imagine that Butler and The Buhl saw the handwriting on the wall and came to their senses. They probably realized they could no longer endure the damage Lacey's unpopular and unproductive stance was inflicting on their entire operation, so they had to stop the bleeding.

He said, "You all were a well-oiled machine, hard as nails, armed to the teeth with community support, and weren't about to back down. Consequently, besides having been ordered to do so, they took their only way out to save their skins. They capitulated to all of your demands. Ted," he said, turning to him, "you have normal authority as general manager, and you may appoint whomever you want for any position."

"Where does that leave Lacey in this equation?" Mitch asked.

"I have no idea. Actually, the question is irrelevant and shouldn't be of any concern to you. Just go and perform the jobs for which you struck. Now, that's a wrap."

Smiles broadened on the strikers' faces. Lacey's house of cards had crumbled completely. Our peaceful sit-in had worked. We'd pulled off a people's victory, a *coup de grace*, an ultimate justification of our faith; and radio history was made. If there was ever an occasion to celebrate, this was it. In our glory, we drank in the joy of victory and bowed our heads, our hands locked together.

"...With our faith. We believed. We knew. And we thank You Father."

I left the celebration and went to my office. There I sat and took a few moments in memory of my loving and caring mother. I'd never forget the many hours she'd spent with me, planting the seeds to prepare me to face and deal with the challenges of the real world. I knew she would've been happy and proud of me. I thanked God for blessing me with Mother Dear, and then returned to the lobby and joined the others in jubilation.

The station signed back on the air at 4:15 PM.

Lacey had dug a hole from which he couldn't extract himself. His lifelong quest for absolute power and control turned out to be his downfall. Three weeks later, he finally met his defeat when he and Moonman were sent packing.

By now, I had put on the mantle of leadership, spending time with my new recruits, going over the homework I had given them. Because many of the agencies now used Arbitron's radio audience estimates in making their buys, I taught them to decipher it. In addition, I instructed them on how to find demographics in the Black market, locally and nationally, and other nuances of salesmanship.

Meanwhile, the faces in positions of influence at many of the big agencies were changing almost daily. While a few young male buyers were moving up in their agencies, more than a few were leaving for other agencies, or starting up their own.

Now the Women's Movement was breaking the "glass ceiling." Former secretaries and receptionists whom I'd befriended through the years were finding opportunities to become radio time salespeople or agency buyers, and those buyers gave me more solid influence at their level, and even helped with "ins" to their superiors.

Moreover, Black agencies emerged on Madison Avenue – Junius Edwards, Howard Saunders, Zebra, John Smalls and Uni World. And with the rising status of the Black Market, Proctor, a good friend of mine, was working with the vice president of Campbell Ewald as coordinator for the American Association of Advertising Agencies' special course called "Careers in Advertising for Minorities." It was designed to train Blacks to qualify for staff level jobs that would eventually bring about some Black input at the agency level.

In entertainment, with the success of Melvin Van Peebles' "Sweet Sweetback's Baadassss Song" and "Super Fly," a stream of blaxploitation flicks hit the city. They gave the Metro Theater Chain and the Fox Theater (both staunch supporters of my market) the chance to make money and revitalize a part of downtown Detroit.

At the same time, Motown, Gamble'n'Huff, and Stax records were capturing top spots in the top forty picks. Black music could no longer be denied. Some white stations were falling in line and rearranged their music formats to include soul.

More than a few white record companies set up special marketing departments to promote their Black artists to take advantage of soul's rising popularity among the general populace. With these events, The Tower was cashing in almost exclusively, airing those companies' spot-sell promotions, their co-op buys for record stores, and their spot-sells tagging their artists' appearances at nightclubs and concerts.

I fostered the spiral of changes and took advantage of the new attitude that was now accepting my market as real and viable. In the past, The Tower's business only scratched the surface; now it was commanding business throughout both the advertising and entertainment industries.

With each of my new salesmen, I crisscrossed the suburbs, introducing them to agencies and clients, watching them make presentations, and in some cases, picking up orders. Only when I was completely comfortable with each one's progress and performance did I cut him loose to go out on his own.

Several months later on a beautiful afternoon in '72, I was driving back to The Tower, as sighs of the summer breeze crossed my body. While dancing in my seat to Marvin Gaye's "What's Going On," when, suddenly, the music stopped, as did my exuberance. I listened.

"This is Ted Dawson, General Manager of WTOP. It gives me extreme pleasure to be able to bring to you, the people, and our monthly editorial on our progress here since you so gallantly supported our struggle for Black management. First, I want to dispel the rumors now circulating in the community that Black management has discarded the original purpose of the strike and is now caving in to ownership's whims. That is entirely untrue. So let me set the record straight on what's been done here since the onerous clouds of frustration were lifted from our shoulders.

"The blending of our style of management into The Tower's system has finally made it community-oriented. We've incorporated healthy Black features into our daily format such as The Word, Drumbeat, Black history contests, Black sport features, and the Black Community Calendar. We've also established programs for community leaders to debate issues of high interest. Our news department is no longer a rip'n'read operation. It no longer has to receive permission to air Black news items from an insensitive and uninformed management. We've become the source for the dissemination of our community news. Anything and everything breaking in the community is brought to our attention, and if it's credible, it's aired on the next newscast.

"With the hundreds of letters we've received suggesting topics to explore, I'm pleased to announce there are other improvements in the mix. So please ignore any rumors and continue to stay in touch with us. Without you, our listeners, we wouldn't be here. For the very first time many in the community now views The Tower, as an entity in itself. No longer is it referred to as Her Majesty's station, or that of any other air personality. It now stands as its call letters spell out: WTOP,The Tower Of Power! This is Ted Dawson. Thank you."

With my goal accomplished, a smile of heartfelt satisfaction crossed my face as I turned my ride onto the freeway.

THE END

Printed in the United States
59633LVS00002B/466-516

9 781424 140206